The Mobile Library

ALSO BY IAN SANSOM
FROM CLIPPER LARGE PRINT

The Mobile Library: The Case of the Missing
Books

This title is also available as an unabridged audio-book
from CLIPPER AUDIO

The Mobile Library

MR DIXON DISAPPEARS

Ian Sansom

W F HOWES LTD

This large print edition published in 2007 by
W F Howes Ltd
Unit 4, Rearsby Business Park, Gaddesby Lane,
Rearsby, Leicester LE7 4YH

1 3 5 7 9 10 8 6 4 2

First published in the United Kingdom in 2006
by Harper Perennial

A CIP catalogue record for this book is available
from the British Library

ISBN 978 1 84632 937 1

Typeset by Palimpsest Book Production Limited,
Grangemouth, Stirlingshire
Printed and bound in Great Britain
by Antony Rowe Ltd, Chippenham, Wilts.

For Sean
2005–2006
R.I.P.

CHAPTER 1

He was sick of the excuses and the lies. He was tired of the evasions and the untruths, of people refusing to stand up and speak the truth and take responsibility for their own actions. It seemed to him like yet another symptom of the decline of Western civilisation; of chaos; and climate change; and environmental disaster; and war; disease; famine; oppression; the eternal slow slide down and down and down. It was entropy, nemesis, apotheosis, imminent apocalypse and sheer bad manners all rolled into one.

People were not returning their library books on time.

'I'm sorry, I forgot,' people would say.

And, 'I've been in hospital.'

Or, 'I liked it so much I lent it to my sister.' (Or my brother, or my mother, or my father, or my cousin, or my friend, who lives up country, or in Derry, or over there in England, actually, and isn't that where you're from?)

Or, 'Sure, I brought it back already.'

Or, 'No. I don't think so. I never had that one out.'

Or, 'I put it back on the shelves myself. Some other one must have it out now.'

Or, 'Someone stole it.'

Or, 'I left it on the bus.' Or in the bath, or on holiday, or in the car and it's in for servicing.

And, even, once, 'It was a bad book, full of bad language and bad people doing bad things, so I threw it away.' (Well, what the hell did Mrs Onions expect, borrowing *Last Exit to Brooklyn*? Israel had asked her, after he'd got her to pay the replacement cost of the book, and a fine, and had steered her safely back towards her usual large-print romantic fiction, and it turned out she had a cousin who'd emigrated to New York back in the sixties and she'd never visited and she was toying with the idea of a trip over for her seventieth birthday and she'd wanted to find out what it was like over there, and frankly, there was no chance of her visiting now after reading that filth, they were going to go to Donegal for a few days instead, to see her sister, down in Gweedore, which was quite far enough, and did Israel know if Frank McCourt had written any others?)

But mostly when they were challenged about their overdue or unreturned books, the good people of Tumdrum would just narrow their eyes and look at you with a blank expression and purse their lips and say, 'Book? What book?'

It wasn't funny. It was cracking him up.

He patted his face with cold water and stared

2

at himself, freshly shaved, in the mirror hung on a nail above the makeshift sink.

He squinted at himself.

In his teens and even into his early twenties Israel had spent a lot of time looking into mirrors, trying to work out whether he was good-looking or not, which was quite a project, a hobby almost; he could have spent hours at it. Was his nose perhaps a little too large, his eyes a little too narrow, his lips too full, his ears not quite right? Pressing, important and immense as those questions had once appeared to be, they no longer seemed to bother him, he didn't know why – he supposed that maybe there comes a time in every man's life when he makes up his mind and decides one way or another about the cut of his own jib and has to learn to live with it, and maybe he'd reached that point, or maybe Tumdrum had just cured him of himself. Either way, it didn't seem to bother him any more, the question of whether he was good-looking or not. What bothered him now was: am I there at all? Or, where am I? He often found himself glancing at himself in the wing-mirror of the van, trying to catch himself out, trying to locate himself, checking for signs of life.

He tried to think who it was he reminded himself of: his father? No. Not his father. Israel was too wide and too plush, too messy: the glasses; the nose; the unruly hair. His dad had always been well turned-out; he was more sports-casual, his dad. Israel reminded himself more of the father of one of his best friends from school, a man who was an art lecturer at a sixth-form college, a tense, fragile, bitter man who wore cords during the week and who had books in the house and who sometimes listened to jazz and blues, and who drank wine to excess, and because Israel's own dad was just a boring old accountant and a moderate man and pretty much happy with his lot in life and with his pastel pullovers and his slacks, it was this stubbly, corduroy-wearing, French-film-watching saddo who had come to represent what Israel thought of as the fully-formed adult male: a copy of Miles Davis's *Kind of Blue* and empty wine bottles and the smell of freshly ground coffee; his friend's dad had made north London seem like the Left Bank, which was where Israel had always assumed he would end up himself, sitting at a café table eating croissants and writing meditative works of philosophy.

But instead he was here, in Tumdrum, in his lodgings, in the converted chicken coop on the Devines' farm, and he looked down at the ground, down past his big white buttery belly and his cords – an old pair of Mr Devine's, phosphorescent cords, cords with a nap and shine like the glint of green on mouldy ham – and there were empty wine bottles stacked everywhere in the room, under the bed and on the dresser – Tumdrum not having yet caught up with recycling – and he had to admit, as he was getting older he was becoming partial to a bit of Miles Davis himself, and he

4

liked his coffee in the mornings just so, if he could have got hold of fresh coffee in the mornings. He wasn't even thirty and he'd become his best friend's dad.

He prodded his little round glasses up onto his forehead and rubbed his chin: it felt horrible, like touching a slightly damp shrink-wrapped skinless chicken breast from Marks and Spencer; not that he had touched a shrink-wrapped skinless chicken breast from Marks and Spencer for a long time, what with being a vegetarian and also being stuck in the middle of the middle of nowhere in the north of the north of Northern Ireland and having to drive around in a mobile library which by rights should have been scrapped and made into a novelty public sculpture years ago.

So, god.

He was still here, Israel Armstrong, BA (Hons), and just about the only thing that was keeping him sane was lovely Rosie, Rosie Hart from the First and Last, who'd been helping him out on the mobile in an unofficial capacity. It was a casual sort of arrangement, but it seemed to work. On the days when Ted was busy with his taxi firm ('Ted's Cabs: If You Want To Get There, Call the Bear'), Rosie would come in and give Israel a hand, and help him get loaded up, and sort out the tickets and clear out the van, and help him find the service points and issue the books, and she was in many ways the ideal helpmeet and librarian: she was young and presentable, and she

5

didn't eat garlic, or shake, or suffer from dyspepsia, or rage, or otherwise exhibit any eccentric or anti-social behaviours, and her bartending experience meant that she was fair but firm and she had an instinctive way with people, while Israel, on the other hand, could sometimes come across as a little . . . brusque. He knew it himself. He wasn't proud of it.

If someone came in to the mobile, for instance, a borrower – or a 'customer' as Linda Wei, Deputy Head of Entertainment, Leisure and Community Services at Tumdrum and District Council insisted on calling them – and they asked for a book, Israel would always start out with good intentions. He'd say, 'Hello! Welcome!' and try to be as cheery as a mobile librarian might reasonably be expected to be, and he might even ask the person if they knew the title of the book they were after, but invariably the person – let's call them Mrs Onions, for the sake of example – would say 'No,' and Israel might manage to remain patient for a moment or two and he might say, 'OK, fine, do you know the name of the author?' but then of course the person – let's say still they're Mrs Onions – would say, 'Och, no,' and Israel would start to struggle a little bit then and the person, Mrs Onions would usually add, 'But you'd know it when you saw it, because it's got a blue sort of a cover, and my cousin had it out last year I think it was, and it's about this big . . .', at which point Israel would lose interest completely, would be incapable of offering anything but his illdisguised north London university-educated liberal scorn for someone who didn't know what they wanted and didn't know how to get it. But Rosie, Rosie would take it all in her stride and she'd try to find every blue-coloured book in the van and if they didn't have it in, sure they could get a few blue-coloured books on inter-library loan, it was no problem at all. Israel just couldn't be bothered with all that; Israel liked the idea of public service, but he struggled with being an actual public servant.

Rosie, though, she was a saviour. She was really something special, Rosie. Israel liked Rosie a lot; he couldn't deny it. She reminded him of someone. She reminded him of his girlfriend, in fact, Gloria, back home in England.

There were of course things about Rosie that Israel didn't like; you couldn't spend much time with someone on a mobile library and not get annoyed and irritated by their little tics and habits. The mobile library after all was really no more than a giant rabbit hutch, or a book-lined prison cell, a place of strictly limited human dimensions; you couldn't wave your hands around too much in the mobile without knocking something over. In the mobile library you lived life, but in miniature, and you minded any hot liquids.

Israel didn't like the way Rosie ate chocolate, for one thing: the way she'd just pop a piece of chocolate in her mouth, and cheap chocolate too, and munch on it like a chipmunk, unapologetic, and so fast. Back home in London Gloria never really ate chocolate— 'A moment on the lips, a lifetime on the hips,' she'd say patting her little wasp-like waist – and if she ever did eat chocolate, she only ever ate Green and Black's, a tiny little square. Rosie also had the habit of applying her make-up in the library, even when there were borrowers in, as if she were in the privacy of her own home; Gloria would never have done anything like that. Israel had lived with Gloria for – what? – four years before coming here and he had never seen her apply her make-up in public. He wondered, now; thinking about it, if she had some kind of magic make-up that never needed reapplying. Or maybe he just wasn't paying attention.

Rosie also smoked and chewed her fingernails, and these were bad habits by any standards, but Israel didn't mind; his were only mild dislikes, after all, in the grand scheme of things, and they were consistently outweighed by the many things he did like about Rosie. He liked the fact that she had a slightly bloodshot right eye, for example, which she claimed was from having suppressed a sneeze and burst a blood-vessel, and which made her look . . . interesting. He liked the fact that she never finished a novel, that she would jump around from book to book, and would fold down the corners and cram the books into her shoulder-bag, wrinkling and wrecking the covers – *Memoirs of a Geisha* covered in lipstick and crushed to a pulp – because he would never have done anything like that himself; he'd always been a completionist; he had to finish a book once he'd started it; it seemed like bad manners not to, like not finishing the food on your plate.

Rosie was a breath of fresh air.

'Why do people read all this rubbish?' he'd complain when they were issuing books.

'Relax, Is,' she would say. She always called him Is – and he liked that too. 'Who cares?'

'Do people not want to improve themselves though?' he'd say.

'Not necessarily. People don't just read books to improve themselves.'

'Well, they should do. They should be reading Emerson or Thoreau or something.'

'Why?' she'd say. 'What did they write?'

'Books!' he'd say. 'Important books!'

'And are they dead?'

'Yes, of course!'

'Well, there you are then. No one wants to read books by dead people.'

'What?'

'It's depressing.'

'It's not depressing. It's . . . that's . . . Two thousand years of human civilisation.'

'Live and let live,' Rosie would say. 'You can read Everton and Throw if you want.'

'Emerson and Thoreau.'

'Yeah. Right. Tea?' she'd say.

And, 'OK, yeah,' he'd say, defeated, and that would be that.

He liked the way Rosie drank her tea and coffee. He liked her broad swimmer's shoulders, and her hippyish kind of dresses. He liked the way she tucked her thick dark hair behind her ears, and the way sometimes when he arrived for her in the van she still had the towel around her head where she'd washed her hair, and she'd come anyway, drying her hair as they went. He liked the way they'd be sitting in the van and waiting for a borrower, and they'd just talk and time would pass. And he liked . . . Well, he liked her a lot.

Not that there was anything between them. There was *absolutely nothing* between Israel and Rosie. It was important to make that clear. Rosie had an ex, the father of her son, Conor, and Israel had Gloria – who was coming over to stay next weekend, coming all the way over, finally, finding time in her busy schedule.

Israel and Rosie were just good friends.

He glanced at his watch, pulled on a T-shirt and his old tank-top, which he noticed was becoming a little ruched around the waist – it needed a wash – and as he shrugged on his duffle coat and did up his old brown brogues he had to admit maybe it wasn't such a bad life.

He was paid to drive around beautiful, rural, coastal Irish countryside, with a van full of books and pleasant female company. Maybe life as an English, Jewish vegetarian, corduroy-wearing mobile librarian on the north coast of the north of Northern Ireland wasn't so bad after all.

Look at yourself, Armstrong, he told himself, with a last glance in the mirror: you have nothing to complain about. Really, you don't.

And he didn't.

Until, that is, the disappearance of Mr Dixon from the Department Store at the End of the World.

CHAPTER 2

It started with an argument. It was too early for an argument, far, far too early.

'What d'ye think yer doin'?'

'Sorry?' It caught Israel off-guard.

'Ye deaf, or what?'

'No,' said Israel. 'No. I am not deaf.'

'Well then.'

'Sorry?'

Israel had the window wound down, and was staring the man full in the face, and the man did not look happy. Indeed, Israel guessed the man might never look happy; he had a profoundly unhappy kind of a look about him: it was the shaven head and the pierced eyebrow and the nicotine lips and the cigarette tucked behind his ear, and the Manchester United football shirt pulled tight over a hard-looking, family-haggis-sized pot-belly, and the dark, cynical look in his eyes. He looked like a man who woke up angry and went to bed incandescent.

'Look, you've totally lost me I'm afraid,' said Israel.

'*What*. Do. *You*. Think. *You*. Are. *Doing*?'

'I'm parking, which is not that easy, actually, without power steering and—'

'Aye, all right, well, you can't park there.'

Israel had pulled up the mobile library next to a large silver Mercedes.

'Sorry, I—'

'Ye blind?'

'No. I am not blind. And I am not deaf, I—'

'Can ye not raid then?'

'Sorry. I didn't catch that. Can I . . .'

'Can ye raid?'

'Raid?'

'Aye, raid.'

'Read?'

'Aye.'

'Read? Ah, read. Yes. Thank you. I can read, actually. In fact, as you'll see, I'm driving the—'

'Aye, right. So you'll see that's a reserved space. See, says here "RESERVED".'

'I just thought—'

'Aye, well, you thought wrong.'

'Couldn't I just park here until—'

'No.'

'But—'

'These spaces are reserved.'

'Yes, but it's only—'

'I just said no. What's the matter with ye? D'ye think I'm joking?'

The man had little flecks of spit – the real thing, real threat-phlegm, the stuff of demented dogs and monkeys – around his mouth, Israel noticed.

'No. No. I don't, actually. I don't think you're—'

'Aye, right. Well. Move yerself on in this piece of crap.' He pronounced crap as though with a double k.

'But—'

'Move. Her. On.'

'OK. Fine. Sorry. Look.' Israel stuck his hand out of the window in a rather feeble, placatory, let's-shake-hands-and-make-up kind of a gesture. 'I feel we've maybe got off on the wrong foot here. I'm Israel Armstrong.'

The man ignored his hand. 'I know who you are. You were meant to be here half an hour ago.'

'Ah, yes, few problems with the mobile on the way over. You must be the caretaker—'

'Round the back.'

'Sorry?'

'Round. The. Back. You. Can. Parkee. Upee. Round. The. Back. Do. You. Understand?'

'Yes.'

'Aye, right. Good. I'll go open her up for you.'

Oh, God.

Israel was getting a headache. He didn't always have a headache these days – just every other day. Because, honestly, he was getting used to life around Tumdrum, he really was. Like a prisoner eventually becomes accustomed to his captors, and adults as they get older eventually have to learn to live with some slight stiffness and joint pain in the morning and a sense of perhaps having lost their way a little on the road towards manifest destiny.

'Move!'

'Yes. Just going,' said Israel, grinding the gears.

And he was certainly getting used to the colourful locals and their charming and eccentric ways.

He hadn't had any breakfast, that was Israel's problem, a cup of tea before he left the Devines' farm, which was hardly enough to sustain a growing young man like himself. Israel had lost a little weight since arriving in Tumdrum, due to the lack of readily available non-meat protein, but he still clocked in at a solid 36-inch waist and 16 stone, not hideously fat by any means, but big enough for people to refer to him as 'big lad' and to mean it. He'd worked up a sweat already this morning and could have done with a nice fried egg soda or maybe a big bowl of porridge with the cream off the milk. Or some Tayto cheese and onion crisps. Or maybe a nice croissant. No, don't get him started on croissants, or *pains au chocolat*, or muffins: Israel fantasised about breakfast pastries. Fresh breakfast pastries were not readily available in and around Tumdrum, although the baker's, the Trusty Crusty, did do a nice cinnamon scone; scones were about the closest thing Tumdrum had to fresh patisserie items.

He'd been working hard, up until midnight and up again since six, getting the van loaded. Today was the big day. Easter Saturday. Today was the first day of Israel's first ever mobile library touring exhibition, his debut as keeper and curator of

Tumdrum's heritage and history. Today was the day when Israel got to unveil Tumdrum and District's mobile-library-sponsored five-panel display showing the history of the famous Dixon and Pickering's department store, which was celebrating one hundred years of serving Tumdrum and District, and indeed the whole of the north coast of the north of Ireland and beyond, keeping the local farmers and their wives supplied with polyester-cotton sheets, Royal Doulton figurines, and Early Bird Light Suppers in the Cosy Nook, the award-winning cafeteria on the first floor, where on a clear day it was possible to see Scotland while you ate your jumbo gammon panini (served with chips and a light salad garnish).

It might not seem like it to you or me, and it certainly wouldn't have seemed like it to Israel six months ago, but today was the real deal, a genuine event, a happening around Tumdrum. Dixon and Pickering's was about as famous locally as the Giant's Causeway a little further up round the coast: it was the Harrods, the Selfridges, the Fortnum and Mason, the Macy's, the Tiffany's, the Woolworths and the Wal-Mart of North Antrim all under one roof, and it had survived and thrived where other family-owned department stores had failed; it had made it to one hundred. And now it was none other than Israel Armstrong, mobile librarian, who had been tasked and commissioned to help the store to commemorate the occasion in style.

Israel couldn't deny it: he was honoured. And he also couldn't deny it: he was maybe going soft in the head.

He drove round the side of the building to the back.

It was undoubtedly a lovely spot, right by the sea. Actually, it wasn't *by* the sea, that didn't do it justice: you couldn't really say that Dixon and Pickering's was by the sea; Dixon and Pickering's was *on* the sea.

Dixon and Pickering's official motto – which was printed boldly on all the shop's plastic carrier bags, just below the company crest, an image of a lamb lying down with a lion in a bucolic scene also featuring fauns and nymphs frolicking beneath mountains by the sea – was 'The Customer Is Always Right', which was wrong, actually, in Israel's experience round about Tumdrum and in Northern Ireland generally. In his experience around here the customer was almost always wrong, unless you wanted to make a big deal about it, in which case the motto should really be amended to 'The Customer Is Always Right . . . Eventually', or '. . . After Threat of Legal Action'.

Dixon and Pickering's was known locally as the Department Store at the End of the World, which was an accurate description, in several senses: you could have picked up Dixon and Pickering's and plonked it down off a dirt-track near an old gold-prospecting town in the middle of Alaska or in some as-yet-undeveloped remote province in

China, and people wouldn't have blinked an eye; put moose or fried rice on the menu in the Cosy Nook and it would have fitted in just fine; because for all its airs and graces Dixon and Pickering's remained an outback kind of shopping experience.

Built in 1906, Dixon and Pickering's still stocked items that other department stores had stopped selling quite some time back, around about the Second World War in fact – his and hers thermal underwear, and two-colour sock wool, and a full range of hearth-sets, and extending toast forks, and wind-up repeater alarm clocks, and paraffin lamps – and it looked as though, with a slight push, you might be able to topple this whole teetering mound of old stucco and kitsch and knick-knacks and watch it disappear under the Irish Sea's big white waves. On a rough day the salt spray came right up over the stone walls of the car park and lashed at the store's stone steps and the new disabled access ramp. People said that if you were to shop in Dixon and Pickering's just once a week and parked down at the sea wall then your car would be gone in a year, eaten alive by salt and rust, like the proverbial cow in a bottle of Coke.

The building itself was three storeys high, wide and spreading, and painted a lurid carnation pink, with palm trees planted all round it: it reminded Israel of a giant plate of salmon blini with chives, and it certainly looked as though it belonged somewhere else, in Miami maybe, or on a fully loaded side table at a north London bar mitzvah party, and definitely not on the lonely north coast of Ireland.

There was absolutely no doubt about it: Dixon and Pickering's was unique. Dixon and Pickering's was undoubtedly – as one of the titles on the helpful A3-size laminated sheets of Israel's five-panel touring exhibition pointed out – A Landmark and A Legend.

Israel parked up.

It was raining, of course. It was always raining in Tumdrum. Even if it wasn't raining, not at that *actual* moment, then it was getting ready to rain, biding its time, waiting until you'd left the house without your coat and umbrella and you were more than halfway to wherever it was you were going so it was too late to turn back, and then whoosh!, suddenly you were wet right through.

It rained here all the time, but still it somehow caught you unawares, creeping up on you. If it was possible for weather to be duplicitous and under-mining, then Tumdrum's weather was: it was *bad* weather, morally bad weather; it was rain that left no visible trace, no puddles, only a deep-down damp, a remorseless damp that at first you couldn't get out of your clothes and then you couldn't scrub out of your skin and then you couldn't dig out of your soul; the kind of damp that if you could have smoked it, you wouldn't have known but already you'd be addicted.

And what was worse even than the soul-destroying rain was that around Tumdrum the sky always seemed to be the colour of the road and the road was always the colour of the sky, a grey, grey, grey, one of a million shades of grey that Israel knew by heart by now, and today, this morning, it still being early, the sky was a kind of beige grey, like the trim in the interior of a particularly nasty 1970s sports car, the shade of a soulless future.

The caretaker emerged from the back of the store and into the rain and waved Israel over.

'Come on ahead then. I'll show you where you're setting up.'

'Would you mind, just . . .' Israel turned up the hood on his duffle coat and half-heartedly indicated back towards the van, to the bags of poles and panels for the display, but the caretaker had gone already. So Israel followed him up the stone steps and inside the famous big pink building.

The back entrance took you in through kitchenware and hardware, Panasonic bread-makers to the left of you, pop-up gazebos and battery display stands to the right. A worn but clean red carpet led through the store, up past linen and beds, skirting contemporary furniture and on through greetings cards, stationery, board games and leather goods until finally you reached the front entrance to the store, where, as is traditional, you could purchase gifts, watches, jewellery and crystal at the foot of a wide staircase which took you up to ladies' fashions and accessories.

'Here's you,' said the caretaker, indicating a tiny space between the sweeping staircase and a jumble of glass display cases featuring vases, decanters and earrings.

'I don't know if I'll be able to squeeze everything . . .'

But the caretaker had gone.

Right, thanks.

Israel trudged back through the store – he was trudging because his old brown brogues were slowly breaking down, widening and splitting, the leather uppers and the smooth leather soles unable to contend with the fast pace, the pounding, and the never-ending dung of country living – and he prepared to unload the exhibition through the disabled access door at the back of the mobile library. Which was easier said than done.

The disabled access door was actually more likely to render you disabled than to ease your access: it was pretty stiff to open, where someone had rear-ended the van at some time, and when you did get it open you had to tie it back with a piece of string because the catch had gone, and the roll-a-ramp itself weighed a ton and was a bugger to fold up and down.

But then the whole van was just like that, and you got used to her eventually, and as long as you watched the oil, and the tyre pressure and the water, and kept her doors lubricated with petroleum jelly, and remembered not to use the full trigger on the petrol pump when you were filling

21

her up, and had a couple of spare alternator belts on board at all times, and as long as you had a dedicated full-time mechanic on hand, then really she was no trouble at all. She took a little more care and maintenance than Israel's mum's old Honda Civic back home in London, but then you couldn't get two thousand books and fully adjustable shelving in a Honda Civic – in fact, as far as Israel remembered, you'd be lucky to be able to get the weekly supermarket shop, a bag of sucky chocolate limes and a handful of CDs in a Honda Civic. To his surprise, Israel seemed to have outgrown little city runabouts. He'd grown accustomed to the van and to her big old-fashioned country ways; he'd got used to grinding the gears, and the uncomfortable, elevated driving position, and he'd grown accustomed to listening out for the little rattles and shakes that meant he needed to get Ted to take a look at the engine before the whole thing blew. As long as Israel didn't have to touch anything mechanical, as long as everything was going smoothly, he was absolutely fine.

He checked his watch. Ted was supposed to be meeting him, but there was no sign of him. He was going to have to do it all by himself.

He eventually dragged all the display poles and panels out of the van and through the store and started setting up.

The caretaker had turned some music on, which was now flooding the huge empty spaces of the store, filling up every little crack, like grains of sand in a picnic or long white worms of Polyfilla from a tube. There was 'Dancing Queen' by ABBA, and Chris De Burgh's 'Lady in Red', and Elton John's 'Candle in the Wind', all played just below tempo, legato, and with humming low chords, each song bleeding into the other, with a generous use of alto sax and what sounded like a flugelhorn, or a muted flugelhorn, or maybe a nose-flute to carry the melody, a sound so mucousy and clotted it made you feel all bunged-up and fluey just hearing it. TV theme-tunes from the 1970s merged seamlessly with pop hits of the 1980s and the Beatles, the slow songs played too fast, and the fast songs played too slow. He had a headache before: now he was actually beginning to feel sick. His hands were sweaty.

When Linda Wei had shown him in her office how to set up the panel display – or the 'Velcro-Compatible Exhibition and Display System', as she insisted on calling it – she'd had it done in minutes, with a cherry scone in hand, and it had looked perfectly simple, but, like most things in life, it turned out only to be simple once you knew how to do it. It took Israel two hands and goodness knows how long of pressing and clicking poles and lifting panels into position to the accompaniment of Boney M, Stevie Wonder, Kris Kristofferson, Celine Dion and the theme from *Miami Vice*, but when he finally got it up it was pretty solid, and if he said so himself his full-colour five-panel display on the history of Dixon and Pickering's looked pretty good. He couldn't deny it, he was proud of his work: on this day, at this moment in time, to his own surprise and doubtless to the amazement of others, if they'd been in the slightest bit interested, Israel Armstrong probably knew more about the history of Dixon and Pickering's than anyone else alive.

He knew all about how the original Mr Dixon, the haberdasher, the man with the vision, had inherited money from a distant relative sent out to seek his fortune in New South Wales, and how he had joined forces with the original Mr Pickering, the milliner, the man with the eye for detail, and how the two of them had dreamt of a department store to rival those of London and Dublin, selling fancy goods and fine china, and wallpaper and animal feed. He knew how they had raised the money for the building from financiers; and how the revolutionary steel-frame building had been constructed partly on site and partly in Glasgow and then shipped over. And he knew all about the original layout of the store, with the little mahogany booths on the ground floor, with William Patterson the Watch Doctor tucked up in one, King's Barber Shop in another, and Mr E. Taylor the Tailor alongside them; and how the booths were replaced in the 1940s with stained-pine counters, and how eventually the whole store had gone open-plan in the sixties, when the oak-panelled entrance hall was remodelled and the revolving door removed and replaced with something state-of-the-art in shiny metal and plastic; and now all that remained inside of the original building was the old staircase. Israel had read and carefully noted down all this information from the archives of the *Impartial Recorder*, and from the old Dixon and Pickering business ledgers now kept in Rathkeltair library, and he had rendered it all lovingly in laminated text and photos, and had pinned it up with his own hand with drawing-pins to the Velcro-Compatible Exhibition and Display System.

And when he stepped back to admire this thing, his handiwork, this Bayeux Tapestry of North Antrim's greatest department store – to the tune of Michael Jackson's 'Beat It' arranged for flute and classical guitar – he saw that it was good.

Unfortunately, though, when he stepped back he also stepped straight into one of the freestanding glass display cases.

Which, to his horror, began to fall, taking with it its display of miniature crystal teddies, china meerkats, porcelain kittens, carved owls and collectable Scottie dogs, elephants and pigs.

And as it fell, it hit another display case.

And then another.

'Oh . . .' began Israel, but didn't have time to finish his sentence as he did his best to prevent a fancy goods domino effect, trying to hold on to toppling cases, but he was too late and by the time the toppling had ceased, five cases were down:

broken bowls and jugs and decanters, carriage clocks, charm bracelets, lockets and little glass candleholders were everywhere.

It was giftware apocalypse. Israel was speechless.

'Beat It' had morphed into John Lennon's 'Imagine'.

The caretaker appeared.

'What the—'

'Sorry,' said Israel.

'Sorry?'

'For the—'

'Forget it.'

'Really?'

Something was wrong here. The caretaker's already ghastly pale and freckled features had turned a ghostly, paler white.

'What's the matter?' asked Israel. 'Are you OK?'

'It's all gone.'

'What's all gone?'

'Everything,' said the caretaker. 'The money. We've been robbed.'

CHAPTER 3

Israel and the caretaker hurried up the big mahogany stairs to the first floor – hurrying past Ladies Fashions, which were mostly XL and pastel, past Accessories, which were mostly scarves and super size handbags, and past the Cosy Nook cafeteria, which was dark and empty and smelt of yesterday's scones and lasagne and milky coffee, and further still, through double doors marked 'Private: Staff Only' – and then up another staircase onto the second floor.

They were in the eaves of the building. It was warm. Downstairs on the ground floor there were high ceilings and chandeliers, but up here, tucked away, it was all fluorescent lights and polystyrene tiling, and there was that eloquent whiff of bleach from the toilets. There were Health and Safety notices on the walls, and whiteboards and pin boards, and water coolers, and computers and reams of paper, and gonks and cards and piles of paper on desks – all the usual paraphernalia of office life.

Israel followed the caretaker through the open-plan area into a smaller private office.

'Oh dear,' said Israel. Chairs were tipped over, paperwork strewn all over the floor. 'This doesn't look good. Signs of a—'

'Struggle,' said the caretaker, his breathing shallow. 'And look here.'

'Where?' said Israel.

'There.'

The caretaker was pointing to a wall safe.

Israel had never seen an actual wall safe before – had never had use for one himself, barely required a wallet in fact – and he was shocked to find that a wall safe in reality looks much like it does in films and in the imagination: a wall safe looks like a little square metal belly-button, small, neat and perfect in the flat expanse of wall.

'Huh,' said Israel.

'Look,' said the caretaker.

Israel went over to the safe, pushed the little door shut, opened it again.

'Double-locking system,' said the caretaker.

'Right. Er . . .'

'Key and combination.'

'Uh-huh. And this is where the money was stolen?'

'Some of it.'

'How much was in there?'

'Few thousand.'

'Ah well,' said Israel breezily, 'big business like this, be able to absorb that, won't it?'

'Come here till I show ye,' said the caretaker, who really did seem to be taking things very badly, who looked like a beaten man, in fact, his whole body and his stomach sagging, and he walked through with Israel into another room off the office.

This room was warmer, and smaller still. There were no windows. And lined up against the back wall were two large metal boxes, like huge American fridges, though without the cold water and ice-dispenser facility – Gloria's family had a big fridge, back home in London, and Israel could never work it properly; he always got ice-cubes all over the floor.

The doors of the safes stood open.

'Wow.'

'These are the deposit safes,' said the caretaker.

'Right.' Israel went over to them. 'Can I?'

'Go ahead.'

Israel peeked inside. He stroked the smooth steel shelves.

'They're empty too then.'

'Aye.'

'But they should be full?'

'Aye.'

'Gosh,' said Israel. He always sounded more English in a crisis. 'So how much money would have been in there?'

The caretaker did not reply.

'How much in these?' repeated Israel, remembering not to add 'my good man' and sound too Lord Peter Wimsey.

'A lot.' The caretaker was ashen-faced.

'OK. And how much exactly is a lot?'

'Ach . . .' The caretaker huffed. 'Difficult to say. You know, Bank Holiday. There might have been farmers in yesterday, might ha' sold a heifer, and that'd be the money for a new dining suite, so.'

'Right. I see. So . . . how much, do you think? Thousands?'

'Tens of thousands.'

'Good grief. That much?'

'Could have been. Busy time of year. These uns take about £100,000 apiece I think.'

'Bloody hell.'

'Aye.'

'Gosh. Well . . .'

Israel looked around the room.

'I just cannae understand it,' said the caretaker. 'All the security. CCTV and alarms and all.'

'The doors look fine,' said Israel. 'It doesn't look as if anyone broke in.'

'I can't find Mr Dixon anywhere,' said the caretaker.

'Well, maybe he's just—'

'He's always in his office by now. He arrives half six, parks up down below.'

'Is that his car out front?' said Israel.

'The Mercedes, aye,' said the caretaker.

'Nice car,' said Israel. 'Maybe he's just gone to the toilet, or—'

'Mr Dixon doesnae go to the toilet at this time,' said the caretaker.

'Right.'

'He doesnae go till eight o'clock.'

'Erm. OK. Gone for a stroll then maybe?'

'He doesnae go for a stroll.'

'Well, maybe he's just popped out. You know, to get a paper or—'

'He wouldnae.'

'Well. OK. So . . .'

'I think something's happened.'

'Well, yes, I'd say that's certainly a—'

'Kidnap, d'ye think?' said the caretaker.

'Well, I wouldn't . . . I'm sure there's a perfectly logical . . . There's not a note or anything, is there?'

'I couldnae see one.'

'Could someone have smuggled him out, past all the security?'

'I don't rightly know.'

'D'you mind if I . . .' Israel indicated the office.

'Go on ahead there.'

'You should ring the police.'

'I've rung 'em already. They'll be here any minute.'

Israel took the opportunity to take a quick look around Mr Dixon's messed-up office, which looked out over the front of the department store.

The office was beige. But it went beyond the average beige: it was a profound beige; its beigeness was total and complete. The furniture in the room – pale cream store cupboards and filing cabinets – was all fitted flush to the walls, and the walls were cream, the carpet was beige, and the table and chairs were a pale, pale pine; if you squinted, it would almost have been as though everything had been erased from the room, as if everything had disappeared. It wasn't just neat and functional – it went beyond that: it was a room that seemed to have vanished.

While the caretaker hovered nervously by the door, shifting from foot to foot in a state of profound agitation, Israel absentmindedly picked up some of the files and paperwork from the floor and put a couple of the chairs back upright; he did like things tidy.

The only real distinguishing feature in the room were the few framed photographs on one wall, showing the various Messrs Dixon and Pickering through the ages, standing outside the store, their arms folded, at first unsmiling, black and white men in bowler hats, and then, later, more recently, grinning, bare-headed men in full colour, as though the whole world and the weather had been warming up and cheering up over the past hundred years. The photograph of the current Mr Dixon showed a man of almost negligible features – a face that would not stand out in a crowd. From all his research into the history of Dixon and Pickering's, Israel knew only this about Mr Dixon: he'd inherited the business from his father, who'd taken it on from his own father, the founder; he wore dark suits and white shirts; and he took his responsibilities seriously. Widely respected in the community, upright and upstanding, Mr

Dixon was someone to whom nothing interesting had ever happened. His office was beige: his life was bland.

The phone rang. Instinctively, Israel reached across the desk and picked it up.

'Hello?'

'Michael? Is that you?'

'No. I'm afraid, I'm . . .'

The phone went dead.

'Who was that?' asked the caretaker. 'The police?'

'I don't know. It was a woman. What's Mr Dixon's first name?'

'Mr Dixon he is to us here just.'

'Right.'

Israel and the caretaker stood silently for a moment and there was the distinct sound of Prince's '1999' being played slowly and purposefully on classical guitar: the muzak that played throughout the store was piped in here too.

He was trying to think straight.

'Right. Right. Erm . . . God. First. Right. Would you mind turning the music off?'

'What?'

'Can you turn the music off?'

'What's the point of that?'

'Because! I can't think. I need to . . .'

'But Mr Dixon likes it on in the morning.'

'But Mr Dixon isn't here and I've got his blood all over my hands!'

The caretaker went to turn off the music.

Israel had never been at the scene of an actual crime before, unless you counted the time he'd sneaked with some friends into a screening of a *Star Wars* film in Whiteley's while another friend distracted the attention of the usherette, or the time he'd taken an extra exercise book from the school supplies cupboard. But that was different. This was your actual true crime.

And he suddenly realised that he was in very big trouble.

'Right, don't move,' said a voice behind Israel. 'Stand where you are. Hands raised above your head.'

It was Sergeant Friel.

'Ah, thank God, Sergeant,' said Israel, turning around, not raising his hands.

'Raise your hands,' repeated Sergeant Friel. He was flanked by two police officers holding guns. And the guns were pointed at Israel. 'Hands!'

Israel raised his hands.

'So, Mr Armstrong,' said Sergeant Friel, half in question, half in statement, and entirely in disbelief. He then slowly stroked his moustache and added, clearly disappointed, 'All right, boys, lower your weapons. It's only the librarian.'

Israel and Sergeant Friel had met on several occasions before, none of them exactly propitious: once when Israel had been mysteriously nearly run over by a speeding car when he'd first arrived in Tumdrum; again a few months later when Israel had caused an obstruction on a public highway by parking the mobile library too close to a corner; and again on a regular monthly basis, on Monday nights, when Sergeant Friel came with Mrs Friel to the mobile library to change their books. (Sergeant Friel had a taste for true crime, Israel recalled – Mrs Friel was more romantic fiction – and you might have thought he'd have liked a bit of a change, Sergeant Friel, given his line of work, though admittedly it was mostly serial killer stuff he was borrowing and in all likelihood there wasn't too much of that in the daily life of a policeman in Tumdrum and District.) They had exchanged cross words across the issue desk on a number of occasions, Israel and the sergeant, which was shocking, really: even the PSNI were no better than anyone else at returning their books on time. Rosie was relaxed about fines, but Israel always made them pay. He was a stickler for the fines, Israel.

And now this was role reversal.

The beige office, which was empty just moments ago, was suddenly filled with men everywhere: police officers in police uniforms, police officers in plain clothes, police officers in white paper-suit uniforms.

Israel didn't know where to look, or what to say. He looked at Sergeant Friel.

'I'm sorry. I can't get my head round this.'

'OK, Mr Armstrong,' said Sergeant Friel. 'What did you say? You can't get your head round it?'

'That's right. I can't get my head round it.'

Sergeant Friel wrote something in a small black notebook.

'OK,' he said. 'What time did you arrive here exactly, Mr Armstrong?'

'Erm . . .'

Sergeant Friel again wrote in his little black book.

'I . . .'

Sergeant Friel wrote something else.

'Are you writing all this down?' said Israel.

'Of course.'

'Why?'

'Because because,' said Sergeant Friel.

'Because of the wonderful things he does?' said Israel.

Sergeant Friel took a note of this remark too.

'You don't have to write that down! That was a joke. That was—'

Sergeant Friel cleared his throat and appeared to be about to deliver a speech.

'I am keeping a contemporaneous record of our conversation, Mr Armstrong. Because we're going to have to take you in for questioning.'

'What?'

'You may have some vital information.'

'But I was just here setting up my exhibition.'

'Your what?'

'My five-panel touring exhibition on the history of Dixon and Pickering's. Downstairs . . .'

'Ah, well.' Sergeant Friel noted this down carefully. 'This is a major crime scene now.'

'But—' began Israel.

Sergeant Friel cleared his throat again and began another speech. 'You do not have to say anything, Mr Armstrong. But it may harm your defence if you do not mention when questioned something which you later rely on in court. And anything you do say may be given in evidence.'

Israel stared at him, wide-eyed. 'What?'

'Do you understand that, Mr Armstrong?'

'Yes. Of course I do. No. I mean, no. I mean . . . What? What are you talking about? You can't take me in for questioning. What about my exhibition? I've worked for months getting all that stuff together.'

'That's hardly important now, is it, Mr Armstrong?'

'It may not be important to you, Sergeant, but I spent months getting those photographs laminated!'

'Aye, well, that's howsoever.' Sergeant Friel was still scribbling in his notebook. 'And if you could speak more slowly and clearly?' He raised a finger. 'And just put these on.'

Another policeman stepped forward and dangled handcuffs in front of Israel.

'What?'

'Handcuffs, please,' said Sergeant Friel.

'Look, if this is because of the fines,' said Israel.

'The what?'

'The library fines. You know. Because you never return your true crime books on time, and now you're persecuting me because—'

'Ach!' said Sergeant Friel, his face reddening around his moustache. 'This is nothing to do with library fines! This is an extremely serious matter, Mr Armstrong, and I suggest you start taking it seriously. There has been a major robbery here, and a suspected kidnapping, and you are on the scene, so we're taking you in. It's really quite simple. Now put these on.'

'No! No.' Israel went to turn away. 'I am not putting on any handcuffs. I haven't done anything wrong.'

'Very well.'

Sergeant Friel nodded at the armed police officers flanking him, who promptly stepped forward and took Israel firmly by the elbows, while Sergeant Friel took the handcuffs and slipped them on Israel, palms inward.

'Hang on!' said Israel. 'Hang on!'

'Billy!' called Sergeant Friel, and one of the white-suited policemen who were filling the room approached Israel.

'Pockets,' said Sergeant Friel, and the white paper-suited policeman started searching Israel's duffle coat pockets.

'What!' shouted Israel. 'What the hell are you . . . ! Hey! Hey!'

He stepped back, and the two armed officers once again moved forward and took him firmly by the elbows. As the white-suited man removed the items from his pockets he gave them to another man in a white paper suit.

'What the hell's he doing?' Israel asked of Sergeant Friel.

'He's Exhibits Officer,' said Sergeant Friel.

'He's what?'

As the Exhibits Officer was handed each item from Israel's pockets he placed them with his surgically gloved fingers in little see-through plastic bags, labelling each with a pen. (The contents of Israel's pockets, as revealed by this process were: two Pentel rollerball pens; some tissues (used); a dog-eared copy of the *London Review of Books*, folded in half and then into quarters, which Israel had been carrying around with him for over six months, and which he fully intended to get round to reading, eventually, if only for the Personal ads at the back; a copy of *Carry On, Jeeves*, which was his current between-service-points reading; a page torn out from last week's *Guardian*, containing an advertisement for the position of senior information assistant at the British Library, a job Israel knew he'd never get but which he might apply for anyway; a Snickers bar, which he'd clearly forgotten about, because if he'd known he'd have eaten it already; and a cassette, sides three and four, from an eight-cassette set of Stephen Fry reading *Harry Potter and the Philosopher's Stone*, which had somehow become separated from the box in the library and which he'd forgotten to reshelve; his mobile phone; and lint, a lot of lint.)

Then they swabbed his hands.

Pockets emptied, hands wiped, Israel was escorted through the offices and down the first set of stairs into the department store, which was filled with policemen, swarming like locusts, and then down the mahogany staircase and out of the front of the building, where none other than Ted Carson happened at that moment to be arriving in his cab, his old Austin Allegro with its illuminated orange bear on the roof ('Ted's Cabs: If You Want To Get There, Call the Bear'). Ted was supposed to have been there over an hour ago, helping Israel set up the exhibition. He was too late now.

Ted wound down his window.

'What's he done now then?' said Ted, as if all he could expect from Israel was trouble, and as though the sight of him being escorted handcuffed by armed police officers was pretty much a normal turn of events.

'Ted!' said Israel.

'Ted,' said Sergeant Friel.

'Brendan. What's the trouble?'

'There's been a theft, Ted. This is a crime scene now.'

'Aye, well,' said Ted, who made the fact of Dixon and Pickering's having turned into a crime scene sound no more interesting than a change in the weather. 'But what's he to do with it?'

'We're to bring him in for questioning.'

'Ach, him?' Ted laughed. 'Are you away in the head, Brendan? He's the librarian, for goodness sake.'

'Aye.'

'And he's English,' added Ted, as if that were some further excuse or a disability.

'Right enough, Ted, but I'm closing this area down.'

Ted got out of the car. His bald head glistened, in the dawn. He drew himself up to his full bearish height, and towered over Sergeant Friel.

'Now, what would you want to be taking him away for, Brendan? We've the exhibition to be sorting here.'

'Sorry, Ted. This is a serious crime.'

'Aye, but he's not going to have anything to do with anything, is he?'

'That's what we're trying to establish, Ted.'

'Come on, Brendan. You wouldnae send him to fetch a loaf, would you? Look at him.'

'Sorry, Ted, we've to get on here.'

'Well, let me come with him then,' said Ted, putting out an arm to block Sergeant Friel's way. 'I'll follow yous in the car.'

'I don't think that'd be a good idea, Ted, would it? You're hardly going to want to be seeing the inside of the station now, are you?'

'Ach, Brendan.'

'This isn't your business now, Ted. You'll be obstructing us if I've to speak to you again.'

Ted dropped his arm.

'Ach, honest to God, Brendan. The boy'll not be able to tell you anything. I mean, look at him. He's not a baldie notion.'

41

'Hello?' said Israel. 'Excuse me?'

'You keep out of this,' said Ted.

'This is serious, Ted,' said Sergeant Friel. 'We're taking him in.'

Sergeant Friel and his accompanying officers began hurrying Israel away.

'Ach. No. Brendan!' shouted Ted. 'Hold on, Brendan! Israel! D'ye have a lawyer, Israel?' called Ted.

'What?' Israel was starting to panic now.

Israel was bundled into an unmarked police car.

'It's all right!' called Ted. 'I'll get on to me cousin. Don't panic, son. We'll have this sorted in two shakes of a lamb's tail.'

CHAPTER 4

He was driven away in the car, Sergeant Friel to the left of him, an armed policeman to his right, another armed policeman up front, and the driver. As they pulled off, Israel saw more policemen sealing off the entrance to Dixon and Pickering's with tape.

'Shutting up shop?'

Sergeant Friel wrote this down.

'Are you writing everything down?'

Sergeant Friel wrote this down.

'You're like my recording angel.'

Sergeant Friel wrote this down.

'Oh, God.'

Sergeant Friel wrote this down.

'That's it. Look.' Israel shut his mouth. 'My lips are sealed. Look. Mm mmmm mm mmm.'

Sergeant Friel wrote this down.

They were driving out of Tumdrum on the coast road, the dark sea up high and fretting beside them. Israel was straining to see in the rear-view mirror, to see if Ted was following in his cab; he didn't seem to be.

'Now, why don't you just tell us what happened,

Israel?' said Sergeant Friel, once they'd cleared the last of the housing estates and were out on the open road.

'What do you mean, what happened?' said Israel. He didn't like the way things were developing. 'Where are we going?'

'You just tell us what happened.'

'Nothing happened. I—'

'We're here to help you, you know.' Sergeant Friel had adopted a horrible, oily, emollient tone, cut through sharply with sarcasm.

'Right,' said Israel, who disliked a tone of sarcastic emollience as much as the next man. 'You're here to help me, and I've been accused of something I didn't do, and handcuffed, and bundled into the back of an unmarked police car—'

'Are you not comfortable, Mr Armstrong?' oozed Sergeant Friel.

'No, I'm not comfortable! I'm squidged up here between you and . . . whatever his name is here, and I have no idea what I'm supposed to have done.'

'Do you want us to speak to anybody?'

'Yes.' Israel wanted to speak to his mother, but he guessed she might not be the best person to help him in these circumstances. He had no idea what his mother would say. And his father – God – his father would be turning in his grave.

'Would you like me to open a window?'

'No.' It was freezing cold.

'Would you like a cigarette?'

'What? No. I don't smoke. Why would I want a cigarette?'

Sergeant Friel wrote all this down. The sea passed silently to their left. Israel was still straining to see if anyone was following the car. They weren't.

Sergeant Friel cleared his throat, a sure sign of his being about to deliver some more of his rehearsed lines.

'What is it now?' said Israel.

'Mr Armstrong. You may have seen me making notes. This is a contemporaneous record of our conversation.'

'Yes,' said Israel, 'I know. You told me already.'

Sergeant Friel held the small black notebook open towards Israel. 'I would like you to read them and tell me if you agree with them.'

It was light outside but it was too dark to read anything clearly in the back of the car.

'I can't read them. It's too dark,' said Israel. 'I can't read anything in this dark.'

'I'll read them to you then, and you can tell me if you agree with them.'

Sergeant Friel began to read.

This really was not good. This was way beyond anything Israel had ever experienced before: being in the back of a car, early in the morning, listening to someone reading out an account of what had happened to you over the past half an hour, but from an entirely different perspective to your own;

it was like being on some kind of extreme creative writing course. Sergeant Friel talked about the police officers present. About handcuffing Israel. About giving Israel a caution. And what made it even more sinister was that the whole story was narrated verbatim, so it was all, 'I said', 'He said', 'I said'. If Israel had been a young American novelist, he could really have made something of this material.

By the time Sergeant Friel had finished reading the notebook to Israel and Israel had refused to agree with it, they had arrived at Rathkeltair central police station, a heavily fortified building which looked like it might have been a work-house in another life, a big grey stone building with menacing chimney stacks, barbed-wire fencing and CCTV cameras strung up all around. Huge metal doors opened as they arrived and they drove round the building to the back entrance, past parked police cars and vast industrial bins.

Israel was getting pretty close to hysterical now as he was led through a long grey corridor to a small grey windowless office, where Sergeant Friel spoke to a uniformed officer behind a desk. It was another bizarre, mind-bogglingly rehearsed scene, like a play within a play.

'As a result of forensic evidence linking him to the scene,' said Sergeant Friel, 'I have arrested this person on suspicion of a robbery and kidnapping.'

'What?' said Israel. 'Forensic evidence? I—'

'You'll get your chance,' said the uniformed officer to Israel. 'Now just listen.'

Sergeant Friel then proceeded to read out the contents of his notebook again and at the end he said, 'Offered, read over, refused to sign.'

'This is totally Kafkaesque, do you know that?' said Israel. Sergeant Friel and the other policeman ignored him. 'Hello? Can you hear me?'

Sergeant Friel added this comment to his notebook and then leant across the desk to a small grey box mounted on the wall, which had a slot; he opened up the notebook to the last page and ceremoniously placed it in the slot, and the machine stamped the book. With bright red ink.

'Have you ever read any Kafka though, honestly?' Israel asked. '"In the Penal Colony"?'

The uniformed officer behind the desk said to Israel, 'Do you understand why you've been arrested?'

'No, I do not. I have absolutely no idea why—'

'You do not understand why you've been arrested?'

'Look. I understand it all right, I'm not an idiot, but I don't agree with it—'

'You have the right to have someone informed,' interrupted the officer. 'You have the right to free legal advice. And a right to read a copy of our code of practice.'

'Your code of practice? Code of practice! What are you, a firm of independent financial advisers?'

If Israel's sense of humour went largely un-appreciated on a daily basis around Tumdrum – and it certainly did – then here in Rathkeltair police station it seemed that he was just about the unfunniest person alive.

'We run a duty solicitor scheme, or I can call a solicitor of your choice. You need to tell me.'

Israel asked them to ring Gloria in London. She'd know what to do: admittedly, she specialised in company law, but it was still the law. She'd sort it out.

'Right, good, am I free to go now?'

He was not free to go now.

He was taken into another small grey window-less room with Sergeant Friel and the armed officers. First they fingerprinted him. Then Sergeant Friel asked Israel to remove his clothes.

'What? Remove my clothes? Oh, come on, you're joking now, are you?'

'No. Can you remove your clothes, please, Mr Armstrong.'

'In here? With all of you standing there?'

'That's correct.'

'And with handcuffs on?' said Israel. 'What am I, Harry fucking Houdini?'

'We'll not have the language, thank you,' said Sergeant Friel. 'We'll take the handcuffs off. But you have to take off your clothes. I'm not taking off your clothes.'

'I don't want you taking off my clothes! No, look. This is getting silly now. I mean . . . Look . . .' Israel did his best to calm himself. 'You've brought me in, that's fine. It's wrong, of course, it's just a big mistake, but . . . But the clothes. That's just—'

'Can you take off your clothes please, Mr Armstrong? I'll remove your handcuffs.'

'But . . . I'm a librarian! I check out your books! You can't just . . .'

He recognised another of the policemen present as a borrower of Hayes car manuals from the library, and he appealed directly to him, as a library user.

'It's me! Look! Me. Israel Armstrong. The librarian!'

The policeman stared back emotionless at Israel. Being a librarian was maybe not going to swing it. Israel could see no easy way out of this.

'Do you know Stanley Milgram?' He was babbling now.

'Clothes, Mr Armstrong.'

'Or the Stanford prison experiment?'

'Clothes, Mr Armstrong.'

'In the Stanford prison experiment, they divided up the volunteers into guards and inmates to see how they behaved.'

'Clothes, please.'

'And the guards behaved like guards. And the inmates behaved like inmates. Have you ever read about that? Have you?'

'Clothes,' said Sergeant Friel.

'And if I do? If I do take them off?'

'Then we'll be able to move on.'

'Really?'

'Yes.'

'Fine. OK.' He was desperate. 'I'll take my clothes off. You all have to turn around though, OK?'

'You turn around,' said Sergeant Friel.

'Oh, all right, I see. Fine. OK. *I'll* turn around. This is ridiculous, you know.'

'Thank you, Mr Armstrong. The quicker you get on with it, the quicker it'll be sorted out. This is for you.' Sergeant Friel handed Israel a one-piece paper suit, with a zip up the front.

'I see. It's like Guantánamo Bay.'

'Och aye. Just like it.'

Once he'd been unhandcuffed and taken off his clothes – the duffle coat, the tank-top, his cords, one of Brownie's T-shirts – 'You Could Have It So Much Better' – Israel put on the paper suit and a pair of plimsolls. His clothes were sealed in see-through plastic bags.

'It chafes.'

'Sorry?' said Sergeant Friel.

'The paper suit. It chafes.'

'Right.'

'So we're done now, are we?'

'No,' said Sergeant Friel. 'Now we need to take a blood sample.'

'What?' said Israel. 'A blood sample? You are joking? No, no, no. Definitely not. You said we were done.'

'I did not say we were done, Mr Armstrong.'

'Oh, yes, you did! You said!'

'We're not done, Mr Armstrong.'

'Come on, that's not fair! You keep moving the goalposts.'

'We are not moving the goalposts, Mr Armstrong. We need to take a blood sample,' said Sergeant Friel.

'No. First I agreed to come here. Then I agreed to take my clothes off. And now you want to take a blood sample? It's like being . . . Brian Keenan, or somebody.'

'Aye?'

'Yes. Or . . . You know, the Birmingham Six.'

'Right enough.'

'This is outrageous! This is Abu Ghraib!'

'No. Mr Armstrong. This is Rathkeltair police station.'

'I'm being illegally detained.'

'No, you're being *legally* detained, Mr Armstrong, in full accordance with the law, and in full accordance with the law we need to take a blood sample.'

'You don't need to take a blood sample!' protested Israel. 'I was only in Dixon and Pickering's setting up my display.'

'Aye, well, you've already said that. But we still need to take a blood sample, so we can eliminate you from our inquiries. And I have to tell you, if you refuse to give it, we have to tell the court you refused. And we ask the court to draw an inference.'

'What? The court?' Israel felt like crying. 'The court! No one mentioned a court before. I'm not going to court!'

'At your current rate, Mr Armstrong, you will be going to a court.'

'I can't go to court!' He didn't just feel like crying now. He was about to cry. 'I haven't done anything wrong.'

'The blood sample please, Mr Armstrong.'

'How much blood do you need?'

'It's just a pin-prick, Mr Armstrong.'

'But, but . . . I don't like needles!'

'Your hair then,' said Sergeant Friel. 'We can take a hair if you'd prefer.'

There was no way Israel was going to agree to give a blood sample, but it didn't look like Sergeant Friel was going to back down, so he agreed to the hair. Sergeant Friel left the room and then re-appeared a few moments later with some tweezers.

'What are they?' said Israel.

'Tweezers,' said Sergeant Friel.

'They're bloody big tweezers!' said Israel.

'Hair?' said Sergeant Friel.

'All right.' Israel nodded.

'We need twelve.'

'Twelve!' said Israel, who thought he might pass out at any moment. 'Twelve! You said *a* hair. *A* hair. One. See! You're doing it again! Moving the goalposts! There's a big difference between *a* hair and twelve hairs, you know! I'll be speaking to my lawyer about this.'

'They're only hairs, Mr Armstrong.'

'Ah, well! Tell that to a . . . bald man!'

'You're not bald, Mr Armstrong.'

'No, no! But I will be at this rate. Twelve hairs!'

'The hairs, please, Mr Armstrong.'

Israel remained silent as they plucked hairs from his head.

The hairs were placed into another self-seal bag.

So by half past ten on Easter Saturday, just three and a half hours after arriving at Dixon and Pickering's to set up his historic five-panel touring display, Israel Armstrong BA (Hons) was sitting plucked, exhausted, confused, and wearing his new white paper suit and plimsolls, in a cell in Rathkeltair police station.

The cell was even smaller than the chicken coop he was staying in at George's farm. There was a concrete plinth with a mattress; a toilet bowl with a push-button flush, no toilet roll; a grey blanket. Grey walls. The grey metal door was scratched with graffiti.

And Israel wasn't feeling at all well. He lay on the mattress on the plinth. It was cold. He drew the blanket up around him.

This was not what was supposed to happen. This was not it at all.

CHAPTER 5

He woke in the dawning light to the merry sound of chickens and machinery outside and he stepped quickly to the door of the chicken coop and took a deep welcome breath of the rich country air: the smell of grass; the smell of silage; the thick, complex smell of several sorts of manure; the smell, it seemed to him, in some strange way, of freedom; the smell of very heaven itself. He was getting used to the country and to country ways. He was also getting fewer headaches these days, he found, and he felt lighter, more alert than he had for years: he could feel himself thriving and growing stronger, feeding on all that good corn and milk and fresh air. He threw back his head, filled his lungs with another blast of the world's sweet morning goodness, then put on his duffle coat and slipped on his shoes and quickly went across the yard to the kitchen, greeting the animals as he went: 'Hello, pigs! Hello, chickens! Hello, world!'

In the kitchen Mr Devine was sitting by the Rayburn, wrapped in his blanket.

'Good morning, Frank!' said Israel.

'Good morning, Israel,' Mr Devine replied. 'A wee drop tay?'

'Aye,' said Israel. 'That'd be grand.'

He poured himself a nice fresh mug of tea from the never-ending pot on the Rayburn, then went back across the courtyard to his room where he lay and read for an hour, a fabulous new novel by a brilliant young author he'd only just discovered and whose work he adored and who seemed to be producing novels almost as quickly as he could read them – varied, strange and beguiling, full of stories. Then finally he got back up out of bed, washed his face in a cool calm bowl of water, got dressed, and went over to the farmhouse again to have breakfast and on entering the kitchen he kissed George warmly on the mouth, and she embraced him, and it seemed to him that he could think of no life pleasanter or more preferable than . . .

Oh, God.

He was dreaming.

Or rather no, not dreaming – it was a nightmare. He wasn't in the chicken coop. He wasn't at the farm at all. He was still in the cell. He must have dropped off to sleep. He'd fallen from one nightmare into another.

He glanced round himself, panicking. Oh, good grief. This was terrible. He was trapped.

He could feel his stomach churning, contracting. He could feel himself beginning to hyperventilate. He needed something to read, to calm his nerves. There was nothing to read. He felt frantic.

He tried reading the graffiti on the walls and on the back of the door. But there wasn't enough, and it was too small, and anyway it was all acronyms defying one another and performing sexual acts on one another, the IRA doing this or that to the UVF, who were doing this or that to the UDA, and the PUP versus the SF, and up the INLA, and down the UFF, and RUC this and PSNI that: where were the great wits and aphorists of County Antrim, for goodness sake? Where were the imprisoned scribes? Where was the Chester Himes and the Malcolm X of the jail cells of Northern Ireland? Where were the Gramscis of Tumdrum and District?

Israel felt half crazed with nothing to read and no prospect of anything to read.

He always had something to read; he always *had* to have something to read: reading calmed him; it did for him what music and television and cigarettes and alcohol seemed to do for other people; it soothed the savage breast, and gave him something to do with his hands and between dinnertime and bed. As a child he'd been a precocious reader, hoovering up books like the pigs on the Devines' farm snuffled up their feed; and as a teenager he had read in a frenzy, reading the one solitary delight and pleasure not only sanctioned but actively encouraged by society and by his parents, an absolute one-off, an exception to the rule, a granting of public esteem not for achievement and worldly gain but for inwardness and the nurturing of whatever it was that constituted a soul.

Everyone loved a great reader. And he'd always loved being a great reader – until recently. Maybe it was just part of getting older, or maybe it was being a librarian, or just being here, but lately he'd found he was becoming suspicious of his own love of books. All that reading – it had started to seem wrong, worthless almost, without purpose.

It seemed abominable, thinking it: thinking about it he felt himself quivering inside.

When he was reading these days it seemed to form only a background hum to what was really going on in his mind, like static or a scratch, like the sound of traffic in a city, or insects in the country. And he'd started to wonder, is literature ever any more than this? Just the faint sound of the flutter of the cockchafer and moth beneath the deafening daily grind? Just the popcorn and Coke accompanying the main feature presentation, *MY EGO, MY LIFE*, in IMAX, in full Technicolor rolling loop and six-channel digital multi-speaker surround-sound, projected onto a domed screen, and with every seat the best seat in the house, and all of them occupied by little old me? Was there anything more to it than that?

He considered the people who were the heaviest borrowers from the mobile library, the people he saw the most of, week in, week out: all the children and their parents, checking out books indiscriminately, picture books and easy-readers, the good and the bad, no discernible difference between them; and the teenagers – the local MP's daughter and some of her friends, some gothy-looking boys – who seemed to be working their way through every Ian McEwan and William Burroughs in the county and who possibly as a consequence seemed more miserable even than the average teen; and the adults, women in and out for romantic fiction and men for military history. And when he considered them all he couldn't honestly say that these people were any more equipped socially or intellectually or emotionally than anyone else; they might possibly have known whether or not Cromwell's troops massacred civilians at Drogheda in the seventeenth century, or about life under the Nazis in the Channel Islands, or exactly which Harry Potter they preferred, on balance, but they were no more polite when challenged about their overdue books than the average borrower, and no more or less keen to pass the time of day with a lowly public servant.

Library users were exactly the same as everyone else, it seemed, and this came as a terrible shock to Israel. He had always believed that reading was good for you, that the more books you read somehow the better you were, the closer to some ideal of human perfection you came, yet if anything his own experience at the library suggested the exact opposite: that reading didn't make you a better person, that it just made you short-sighted, and even less likely than your fellow man or woman to be able to hold a conversation about anything that did not centre around you and your ailments and the state of the weather.

He shivered.

Could all that really be true? Did it matter? That the striving after knowledge, the attempt to understand human minds and human nature, and stories, and narrative shapes and patterns, made you no better a person? That the whole thing was an illusion? That books were not a mirror of nature or a mark of civilisation, but a chimera? That the reading of books was in fact nothing more than a kind of mental knitting, or like the monotonous eating of biscuits, a pleasant way of passing time before you died? All those words about words, and texts about texts, and all nothing more than tiny splashes of ink . . .

Nothing to read: nothing to be read.

His mind was racing in the confined spaces and rotations of the cell; Israel was dizzying himself. The whole world seemed to be wobbling around him. He felt like *The Scream*. He felt like crying. Again. He suddenly thought of his mother looking down at him from a great height.

Oh, God.

And the next thing he knew there was a young Asian man standing over him, shaking him, looking down at him. He wasn't sure if he was dreaming or if this was real. It certainly wasn't his mother.

'Mr Armstrong?'

He rubbed his eyes. His shoulders ached.

This was real. The man was standing with his hands behind his back. He had the beginnings of a beard.

'Hello,' said the man. 'I'm Hussain. From Biggs and Short.'

'What?'

'Your solicitors.'

'I don't have a solicitor.'

'No. Well, I'm your legal representative.'

'No. My girlfriend's going to be helping me out with all that.'

'Is that Gloria Cohen?'

'Yes, that's her.'

'The police were unable to contact her, I'm afraid, sir.'

He knew exactly what he meant: Gloria was always too busy to answer her phone. They might have more luck texting her, but even then they wouldn't be guaranteed a response: 'SPK,' would come the reply, but she wouldn't.

'Well,' continued Mr Hussain, 'anyway, I have been appointed your legal representative. I work for Biggs and Short. Mr Billy Biggs is a cousin of Ted Carson, Mr Armstrong, who I believe you know?'

'Oh, no.' That did not augur well. 'Look,' he continued, 'I really don't want to talk to you about this . . . nonsense.'

'I suggest very strongly that you do, Mr Armstrong. This is really a very serious matter.'

Israel held his head in his hands.

The man was looking down at Israel intently. Israel could feel him looking at him. It was unnerving, like the sense he'd had as a child of God right above his head, being able to see him. The man said, 'Did you do it, Mr Armstrong?'

'What? Did I do what?'

'The police say they've got rather a lot of evidence against you.'

'What evidence?'

'Your prints are all over the safe.'

'My prints? No. No. They're . . . I touched the safes when I arrived because . . . I've explained this to them already. I didn't do it. Of course I didn't do it. I'm a librarian.'

Mr Hussain perched sympathetically on the plinth next to Israel.

'Well,' he said, 'how do you explain it?'

'What?'

'If you didn't do it, why have they arrested you?'

'Because I was there.'

'Why?'

'Because of the five-panel touring exhibition of the history of Dixon and Pickering's.'

Israel then told Hussain everything about what had happened that morning and Hussain listened.

'I see,' he said, when Israel had finished talking.

'Do you?' asked Israel, who suddenly found he needed someone to believe in him.

'I understand what you're saying,' said Hussain.

'That's not the same thing as believing me though, is it?'

'Would you—'

'Do you believe me?'

'It's—'

'You don't believe me, do you? You're supposed to be my bloody solicitor and you don't believe me!'

'Would you like me to accompany you to the interview, Mr Armstrong?'

'What interview?'

'You're going to be interviewed by the police shortly, Mr Armstrong, in connection with the robbery, and you have the right to have your solicitor with you.'

'Oh, God.'

As they were talking, there was a bang at the door and a small window opened and a tray was handed in.

'I took the liberty' said Hussain, gesturing towards the tray.

'What is it?' said Israel.

'It's food and drink,' said Hussain, getting up.

'I'm not hungry,' said Israel. He was hungry. He was starving. But he couldn't eat.

'It's coffee,' said Hussain, offering Israel the tray. 'And scones.'

Scones. Scones. Always bloody scones. Around Tumdrum the scone was regarded not as a snack item or as a luxury, but pretty much as an essential food item; around Tumdrum the scone was a *sine qua non.* And this morning of all mornings Israel could have done with a cup of coffee and a scone.

But even Israel couldn't manage a coffee and a scone this morning: things were really that bad.

So, after Hussain had eaten the scones and drunk the two coffees – 'Are you sure?' he said, starting in on scone two. 'They're really good. They're cinnamon. You're absolutely sure?' – he and Israel were taken into the interview room. Two police officers were present: Sergeant Friel and someone Israel didn't recognise.

The policeman Israel didn't recognise switched on a tape recorder, said his name – Israel didn't quite catch it, was it Doggart? Hoggart? – the date, time and place and then he spoke to Israel. 'Can you introduce yourself for the benefit of the tape?'

Israel said nothing.

Hussain gave Israel a little nudge. Back in the cell, he'd explained to Israel that he needed to cooperate. Any questions he wasn't sure about, Israel was supposed to say, 'No comment.'

But instead Israel said nothing. And so Hussain nudged him again. And still Israel said nothing. So Hussain spoke on his behalf, saying his name. And the police officer told the tape that Israel had refused to speak. There was a chorus of huffing and puffing around the room.

'Where'd he get the name, Israel?' Doggart/Hoggart muttered to Sergeant Friel.

'I don't know.'

'What's that?' said Israel.

'Ah! It speaks!' said Doggart/Hoggart. 'Your name. Where'd you get it?'

'My name?'

'Aye. You didn't get it off a bush, did you?'

'What do you mean, I didn't get it off a bush?'

'Why are you called Israel?'

'Why do you think?'

'I'm asking you.'

'I'm called Israel after Israel, the people of Israel, in the Bible. You've heard of that, I suppose?'

'We have to ask,' said Sergeant Friel, whose mock emollience now seemed like true balm compared to Doggart/Hoggart.

'You are named after the state of Israel in the Middle East?' asked Doggart/Hoggart.

'Yes, that too, I suppose.'

'And what's your connection with the state of Israel, Mr Armstrong?'

'What? I don't have any connection with the state of Israel!'

'You're called Israel and you have no connections with the state of Israel or with the Middle East?'

'No. I don't.'

'So why are you called Israel?'

'I thought I'd just explained! My mother's Jewish, and she thought it was a good idea at the time. It was the 1970s. We had family there. It was all the rage.'

'So, you claim you have no contact with the Middle East and yet you have family there?'

'Yes. Look, what has this got to do with anything? I'm from north London. I'm just called Israel: I'm not an Israeli.'

'I see. And what's the nature of your business here in Northern Ireland?'

'I live here. You know I live here. I work here. I'm the librarian!'

'So, you're an immigrant?'

'What? Well, yes. No. No, I'm not an immigrant. I'm English. I just happen to be here. I've got a job here.'

'And your job of work here?'

'I just told you! I'm the librarian! On the mobile library. Ask Sergeant Friel there, he gets his books out from the library once a month. Do you never get books out of the library?'

Doggart/Hoggart did not look as though he got a lot of books out of the library.

There was a malevolent kind of a pause for a moment then – a pause in which Israel looked pleadingly from the downcast eyes of his solicitor to the downcast eyes of Sergeant Friel and then back again to the hard stare of Doggart/Hoggart, who raised his shoulders and rearranged himself in his chair, clearly preparing for another line of questioning.

'How many counties are there in Ireland, Mr Armstrong?'

'Sorry?'

'I said, how many counties are there in Ireland?'

'Erm . . . I don't know. What's this got to do with anything?'

'Can you name three Glens of Antrim?'

'What?'

'It's funny: you claim you're not an immigrant here, Mr Armstrong, and yet you don't seem to know very much about the country in which you're living.'

'I've only been here—'

'Where was the sash worn?'

'What?'

'I said, where was the sash worn?'

'I have no idea what you're talking about. What is this, twenty questions?'

'Do you speak any Israeli languages, Mr Armstrong?'

'Israeli languages? What are you talking about? What do you mean, Hebrew?'

'Arabic?'

'No, I don't speak Arabic. Or Hebrew. I know about two dozen phrases of Yiddish, and that's it.'

'Yiddish?'

'That's right.'

'What's that, a Jewish language?'

'Oh, God.'

Doggart/Hoggart then reminded Israel the interview was being tape-recorded and might be used in evidence in a court of law.

He went on, 'For the benefit of the tape, do you

understand why you have been arrested, Mr Armstrong?'

Israel had had enough. He decided to give up on the conversation and returned to his earlier tactic and remained silent.

Doggart/Hoggart asked again.

And Israel remained silent.

Doggart/Hoggart said, 'If you refuse to make any comment, an inference may be drawn at court.'

This became the pattern for the rest of the interview: Israel silent, Doggart/Hoggart repeating, 'If you refuse to make any comment, an inference may be drawn at court.'

Then Sergeant Friel had a go. 'Tell me what happened, Israel.'

Israel said nothing.

'If you refuse to make any comment, an inference may be drawn at court.'

At which point Hussain had had enough. He asked permission to halt the interview to confer with his client. The interview was duly halted and Israel was taken to the cell with Hussain to confer.

'What the bloody hell do you think you're doing?' said Hussain.

'I didn't do it!' said Israel. 'And I'm not going to allow them to twist what I say to make it appear as though I did.'

'You need to cooperate with the police, Mr Armstrong.'

'Yeah. Right. I know how these things work.'

'What things?'

'False accusations. Conspiracies.'

'This is not a conspiracy!'

'It is a bloody conspiracy! It's like . . . Princess Diana, and the . . . Kennedy assassination!'

'Mr Armstrong—'

'I'm a librarian! I'm not . . . Lee Harvey Oswald!'

'Mr Armstrong, please. No one's saying you are Lee Harvey Oswald. Whoever you are,' said Hussain, 'if you haven't done it, you have nothing to fear from speaking to the police.'

They returned to the interview room.

The interview recommenced.

'Have you had sufficient time to advise your client?' asked Sergeant Friel. Hussain said that he had. And Doggart/Hoggart started in again.

Israel still said nothing. For five minutes. Ten minutes. Twenty. Half an hour.

The interview was abandoned. The tapes were sealed. Two copies. Israel and Hussain were asked to sign the seal of one copy. Israel refused. A note was made in a notebook: 'Refused to sign.'

Israel was returned to the cell, and he buried his face in the mattress. His mind was in turmoil. Why did they keep asking him about being Jewish? Israel didn't even feel Jewish. He was just . . . Israel. And all that stuff about Ireland? How the hell was he supposed to know anything about Ireland? He only lived here.

Hussain reappeared.

'Good news.'

Israel looked at him.

'The DNA's going to take about a week to process.'

'So?'

'I think we can get you bail. There's no other evidence at the moment to link you to the crime.'

'Oh.'

'This is what you want?'

Israel nodded.

Hussain left and then returned half an hour later with a plain-clothes policeman. Israel was escorted back to another policeman sitting at a desk.

A debate ensued between Hussain, the desk policeman, and the plain-clothes policeman, who expressed a concern as to whether Israel should be granted bail.

'It is my belief that Mr Armstrong would fail to return, due to the seriousness of the offence.'

'My client,' said Hussain, 'has a job. He has ties to the community.'

Israel snorted. Ties to the community! He didn't have ties to this community. Shackles, maybe. But ties? Nothing apart from the bloody library. He had nothing in common with these people. He certainly didn't share a common past with them, nor did he want to. He didn't share their feelings, or their language, apparently, or common assumptions, and he definitely did not share their so-called sense of humour. Ties to the community! For goodness sake.

Hussain continued. 'He has a home.'

Israel snorted again. A home! A chicken coop! That's where he'd bloody ended up here. A chicken coop.

'He is of previous good character.'

Hussain had never met Israel before.

'Also, you have his passport.'

What? Israel didn't know they had his passport. How the hell did they get hold of his passport?

The man behind the desk wrote all this down.

'It is my belief that Mr Armstrong could be a danger to the public,' said the plain-clothes policeman. 'He could commit further offences.'

'My client is prepared to reside at his home, to sign in weekly at the station and to keep a curfew.'

There was a huddle then, and hushed talking between the plain-clothes policeman and the desk policeman, and the next thing Israel knew he was signing forms in triplicate. He glanced at the words. It was an offence, apparently, for him to fail to appear back at the police station in one week. It was an offence for which he could be fined or imprisoned or both.

Then suddenly he was in another room being kitted out in someone else's old clothes and being escorted out past the front counter with Hussain.

'Well, we've got a week,' said Hussain, walking with him down a long grey corridor.

'For what?' said Israel.

'For us to sort all this out,' said Hussain.

'It's not very long,' said Israel.

70

'Well, how long do you need?'

'I don't know.'

'Well, you've got a week. They'll be doing stuff at the forensic science lab. And the DNA database in Birmingham.' Hussain looked at Israel suspiciously. 'They'll also need to prove intent.'

'I didn't have anything to do with it.'

'Fine,' said Hussain. 'You'll be OK then. Here's my card. You understand the bail conditions?'

Israel nodded.

'OK. Well, let's talk tonight. I'll ring you. You can let me know what our next move is.'

Hussain's words rattled in his ear. His next move? His next move?

Israel didn't have a next move.

He had a terrible headache.

CHAPTER 6

Ted had been waiting for Israel in the police station. He was working his way through a giant book of Sudoku puzzles.

'Blinking things,' he said, as Israel shuffled towards him in his borrowed clothes.

'Oh, Ted! God, am I glad to see you.'

'Aye. Well, fancied I'd run into ye – you look like somethin' shot at an' missed, mind.'

'What?'

'And fancy dress, was it?' asked Ted: Israel was dressed in a three-piece pin-striped suit, with a pair of size 11 shoes.

'No.'

'You swap with Coco the Clown?'

Israel was too tired for repartee.

'Aye, well,' continued Ted, 'you look smarter than usual.'

'Thanks.'

'Not that it'd be difficult. Come on, let's get out of here.'

Ted strode quickly towards the doors, Israel following.

'They treat you right?' asked Ted, as they hurried down the ramp.

'God, Ted. No,' said Israel. 'It was awful. It was—' Israel broke off. He found his hands were shaking.

'Aye, all right, son.'

They made it across the yard to Ted's cab.

'D'you get Billy?'

'What?'

'Your brief? My cousin, Billy Biggs, he saw you right?'

'No, no. I got some young bloke called . . . Hussain.'

'Indian fella?'

'I don't know. No. He was from here, I think.'

'He's Indian-looking, but?'

'Well, yes, him.'

'Aye. He's from Belfast. Top of his year at Queen's apparently. Billy swears by him. So?'

'Ted.' Israel stopped walking. 'I think they're trying to frame me.'

'Frame ye?'

'Yes! They're saying I carried out the robbery and the kidnap.'

'Kidnap?'

'Mr Dixon, he's gone missing.'

'Ach.'

'They're trying to blame me for it.'

'Aye. They're just trying to rile ye.'

'Well it certainly worked. Ted, you wouldn't believe the conditions they keep you in.'

'I think I would, boy. Come on, let's go.'

They got into Ted's cab.

Israel found he was shaking so much he couldn't do up his seat belt.

'Ye all right?' asked Ted.

'I don't feel well, Ted.'

'Aye, well, you'll be all right once we're out of here.'

'It's a violation of basic human rights.'

'Ach, Israel.'

'They're framing me, Ted. I really think they are.'

'You're getting carried away now.'

'I am not getting carried away, Ted!' There was a hoarseness to Israel's voice, as though he were about to cry.

'For goodness sake, you're not going to be blubbing now, are ye?'

'No, it was just . . .' Israel swallowed hard and tried to compose himself.

'Look, you're getting yerself all highsterical. Just calm down.'

'But I was in prison, Ted!'

'You were in a police cell. It's no' the same thing at all.'

'But, Ted, what if they manage to pin it on me?'

'Pin it on ye?' Ted laughed. 'What are ye blathering on about now? Pin it on ye? They're not going to pin it on you, son. You're just being silly. You're too sensitive altogether.'

'Too sensitive! Ted . . .' Israel took a deep breath.

'They've arrested me, released me on bail for a crime I didn't commit, and you're telling me I'm too sensitive!'

'Aye, that's exactly right. Get a grip of yerself.'

They drove out of the police compound and into the streets of Rathkeltair. Israel lapsed into silence.

'Linda wants to see you,' said Ted.

'What? Now? Oh, no. Ted, no.'

'Yes.'

'I can't, Ted. Not today. I don't even know what day it is. What day is it?'

'Saturday.'

'She wants to see me on Saturday?'

'I'm afraid so.'

'I can't, Ted. I need to . . . Not now. Not today.'

'You'll be all right.'

'Ted. No. I'm . . . I'm tired.'

'Aye, well. Get the name of rising early and you can lay on till dinnertime.'

'What?'

'It's just a saying.'

'Not now, Ted, please. I need a cup of coffee or something, and something to eat.'

'Aye, right. The old prison food not to your liking, eh?'

They stopped off at the garage and picked up an egg mayonnaise sandwich and a bottle of Coke for Israel, and drove on to Tumdrum.

The food and drink cheered him disproportionately: Israel had never been so glad to eat a triangular-pack egg sandwich and drink a bottle

of Coke in his whole life. And as for Tumdrum . . .
Tumdrum! The sight of Tumdrum, with its outlying
loyalist housing estates, and its little central square,
and the sea down the hill at the bottom of Main
Street, with the car park and the big sewage outlet
pipes spoiling the view, just the sight of it, and the
smell . . . It was . . .

It was wonderful.

Tumdrum! What can you say about Tumdrum?

An impartial observer – and indeed Israel
himself until this morning – might perhaps have
said that the best thing you could say about
Tumdrum was that it wasn't actually offensive,
that it was quite neat, as though a large, plain grey
linen tablecloth had been lain over it and set for
an afternoon tea of bread and butter but no jam,
and that it was plain, plain, plain: the bus stop
with its concrete shelter and seating, the big,
empty flowerbeds, the war memorial featuring
the proverbial unknown soldier, whose rifle and
plaque had long ago turned green, the many
churches and the shops; Atchinson's the Chemist,
with its window display of a plastic set of
cancerous lungs; Byrant's Ladies and Gents
Outfitters, which offered pastel nightgowns and
cardigans protected from the non-existent glare of
the sun by a sheet of wrinkled orange plastic; and
T.M. McGrath's, the grocer, produce displayed
on a small trestle table in its window.

Tumdrum was not really the kind of place that
inspired you to want to stick around for too long;

it was not the kind of place that threw its arms around visitors and offered you a hundred thousand welcomes: it was more the kind of place that made you want to check the bus timetable to find out when the next bus might be leaving and you might be able to wake up from your bad dream; and not until tomorrow, by the look of it.

But to Israel, now, this morning, Tumdrum was like Shangri-la.

'God, it's good to be back,' he said.

'Watch yerself,' said Ted. 'Don't be gettin' all misty-eyed on me now.'

'It's just . . .'

'Aye, all right,' said Ted, with a dismissive wave of his hand. 'Ye ready for Linda?'

'Aye,' said Israel, sighing. 'I suppose.'

'What did you say?' said Ted.

'I don't know,' said Israel. 'I suppose?'

'Ye said "Aye",' said Ted.

'I did not,' said Israel.

'So ye did,' said Ted.

'I did not!' said Israel.

'You're turnin',' said Ted. 'You want to watch yourself. You'll be singing "The Sash" next.'

'The sash!' shouted Israel, leaping up in his seat.

Ted braked. 'What?' he said. 'Holy God. What's the matter with you now?'

'The sash! They asked me about the sash, Ted. Where was the sash worn?'

'What? Who was asking ye?'

'The police were.'

'They were asking you where the sash was worn?'

'Yes. What is the sash?'

Ted cleared his throat.

'You all right?' said Israel.

'Just clearing the pipes,' said Ted, who then began to sing, "It was worn at Derry, Aughrim, Enniskillen and the Boyne."'

'Right,' said Israel, none the wiser. 'And what is it?'

'What?'

'The sash? It's a song, is it?'

'Ach, Israel, you're having me on, are ye?'

'No. They were asking me about it.'

'You'll be asking me next if we're governed from Dublin.'

'No! What was the other thing?'

'Another question?'

'Yes. I know! How many counties are there in Ireland?'

'Counties?'

'Yes.'

'Well, what do ye think?'

'I don't know.'

'In the name of God, boy. We've six. The other lot have twenty-six. Wouldn't ye've thought they'd be satisfied?'

'Right. And can you name the three Glens of Antrim?'

'The three?'

'I think they said three. Are there not three?'

'How long have you been living here?'

'Too long,' said Israel.

'Or not long enough,' said Ted. 'The Green Glens of Antrim are calling to me?'

'Are they?'

'Glenarm, Glenaan, Glenariff.'

'Right.'

'Glencorp, Glenballyeamon, Glendun.'

'Is that it?'

'Glencloy, Glenshesk and Glentaisie.'

'How many's that?'

'Nine.'

'And they all begin with G?'

'Correct.'

'Oh, right.'

They were turning into the council car park.

'What in God's name are they asking you about the Glens for?' said Ted.

'I don't know. They thought I was an immigrant.'

'You are an immigrant, sure.'

'Yes, but not that sort of immigrant.'

'Aye, right, what sort of immigrant are ye then?'

'I'm . . . Well, you know what I mean.'

'Aye, I know exactly what you mean. You think we're predujiced—'

'Prejudiced,' said Israel.

'Predujiced, aye,' said Ted. 'But you're no better yerself, ye know.'

'No, Ted, that's not what I meant.'

'You're still a foreigner to us, ye know.'

'Yes, thanks, I know I'm a foreigner. They kept going on about me being Jewish as well, the police, at this interview. And my name.'

'Why?'

'I don't know,' said Israel.

'It is a funny name,' said Ted.

'It's not a funny name.'

'Sure it is.'

'It's my name.'

'Aye, exactly,' said Ted.

He turned off the engine.

'I tell you what,' said Israel, 'if I was called Ali Akbar I'd probably still be in there now.'

'Don't be daft.'

'I would. I bet if your name wasn't Ted, but . . . Tedinski or . . . Muham . . . ted or something, they'd have you in for questioning.'

'Ach, give over, Israel.'

'Michael Caine, his real name is Maurice Micklewhite, d'you know that?'

'Fascinating,' said Ted. 'Good luck!' And he waved Israel out of the car. 'I'll be waiting.'

Israel went up to the second floor and knocked on Linda's door.

There was no answer, but just as he was about to leave Linda appeared in the corridor. She was wearing a billowing tiger-print blouse, with boot-cut black trousers and high-heeled boots which added at least three inches to her diminutive natural height, raising her to at least five feet tall. She was red-eyed and was clutching a paper tissue in one hand, a paper cup in the other. She looked as though she'd been crying.

'Linda,' said Israel. 'Are you all right?'

'Mr Armstrong,' sniffed Linda. 'Yes, thank you.'

'Er. Good. Well . . .' Israel couldn't think of the next logical supplementary question. He gestured at her paper cup. 'Cappuccino?'

'I wish,' said Linda, dabbing at her eyes. 'I'm on the herbals.'

'Right.'

Linda went into her office, Israel following.

'Peppermint,' she said. 'Did you ever try Atkins?'

'The diet?' said Israel.

'Aye, the diet,' said Linda.

'No,' said Israel.

'Tried it last year,' said Linda mournfully. 'It worked for me. But the wind, honestly.' She gave a little burp, as if in demonstration. 'I lost nearly two stone.'

'Right. Good.'

'Put it all back on again. Missed the scones. Trying this GI thing now.'

'OK.'

'Did you . . . ?' said Linda. 'Sshh.'

Linda raised a finger for Israel to be silent and she gazed around the room suspiciously. Israel followed her gaze. The office was much messier than he remembered – papers and reports everywhere. The plants on the windowsill didn't seem to be thriving.

81

'Sshh. Did you . . . Can you . . . Can you hear anything?' said Linda.

'Like what?' said Israel nervously.

'Just, a wee noise?'

'No. I don't think so. Are you sure you're all right, Linda?'

'Yes. Thank you. The noise though. No noise? Definitely not?'

'No. I don't think so. What sort of noise?'

'A wee sort of squeaking?'

'No. Definitely no squeaking.'

'Hmm. Only, I think I've got a mouse in here.'

'A mouse?'

'Aye. The caretaker says it's because of all the crumbs, see. Haven't been able to catch him so far, the wee blighter. Haven't seen him even. He leaves his droppings, like, but otherwise you'd never know he was there. I can't decide if I can hear him or not.'

'Right.'

'Sending me demented so it is.'

She took a long indraw of breath and slowly got down on her knees and stared at the skirting board.

'Mr Mouse!' she called quietly. 'Mr Mousey! I know you're there!'

'Erm, Linda, shall I . . .'

'Ah,' sighed the crouching Linda. 'It's the mouse, you see, and the diet, and the . . . Honest to God. All these little things, they add up to—'

'Small changes in some variables can cause disproportionate results,' said Israel.

'What?'

'Chaos theory, isn't it? I read a book about it once.'

'Right, I'm sure,' said Linda, distracted.

'Butterfly wings and tornadoes.'

Linda stood up. 'He's a wee hole here somewhere, but I'm damned if I can find it.'

'Uh-huh. Should I perhaps go and come back later, Linda?'

'No! Not at all.' Linda threw back her shoulders and plumped down into her imitation leather swivel seat and took a sip of her herbal tea. 'Anyways,' she said. 'How can I help you?'

'You asked me to come and see you. Ted brought me.'

'Ah, yes. Course. Couple of things. First . . .' She rifled through a teetering pile of papers on her desk, and plucked out a plastic folder. 'Aha! Yes, there's the plan to relaunch all mobile learning centres as Ideas Centres and—'

'What?'

'The Department of Entertainment, Leisure and Community Services have a plan to relaunch all mobile learning centres—'

'Mobile libraries,' said Israel.

'Yes, if you must.' Linda peered over her glasses. 'As Ideas Centres. So they're going to be much more ideas-focused.'

'Ideas-focused?'

'Yes.'

'OK. So when were you going to tell me about this?'

'I'm telling you now, Mr Armstrong.'

'Right. You're just going to repaint the sign on the vans, or . . . what?'

'No, no, no. You'll have to read the report,' said Linda, who seemed to be losing enthusiasm for what she was saying even as she was speaking. 'It's all still blue skies at the moment – we're just throwing things at the wall to see what sticks.'

'Throwing things at the wall?'

'That's right. To see what sticks. But I wanted you to have a glance at the report, see what you think, get your feedback.'

'I think I know what I think about an Ideas Centre, Linda.'

'Yes, well. Let's not rush to judgement, eh? If you wouldn't mind looking at the report and then . . .'

'Yes?'

'Reporting back.'

'OK. If you want me to. That's fine.'

Linda took a long thoughtful slug of her herbal tea.

'Anyway, that was one thing,' she said. 'Point one.'

'Yes?'

'And the other . . . Point two. Is . . .'

'Yes?'

'Is that a suit you're wearing, Mr Armstrong?'

'Yes.'

'Hmm. It's . . . It's smarter, certainly. But maybe a little long in the . . .'

'Yes.'

'Anyway. Where were we?'

'Point two.'

'Point two?' Linda stared at Israel. 'Egg on your chin?'

'Mmm. Yes. Sorry.' Israel wiped it away. 'That was Point two?'

'No! Silly. Point two? Ah, yes! You're in trouble again, I hear.'

'Ah, yes, well—' began Israel.

'Ah, yes, well,' interrupted Linda, who had developed an annoying habit of imitating the way Israel spoke. Ted did it as well, and George. It was like having gone to a new school in a new town and being bullied by the locals, but because Linda was a Chinese Northern Irish woman Israel didn't feel he could reciprocate; and besides, his only Northern Irish accent was a Gerry Adams, which was pretty wide of the mark for a Chinese Northern Irish woman from North Antrim. So he just smiled in response. 'Go on,' said Linda.

So, Israel explained to Linda what he knew about the theft at the department store and Mr Dixon's disappearance, and the fact that his fingerprints were on all the safes, and how they'd come to be there.

Between sips of her tea Linda fixed Israel with a hard stare.

'Well, Mr Armstrong, I'm afraid I do have to ask you this question.'

'Right. Yes.'

'As your line manager, you understand. I have a responsibility.'

'Yes. Fine, Linda. Go ahead. Ask away.'

'Did you steal the money from Dixon and Pickering's?'

'No, Linda. Of course I didn't steal the bloody money from Dixon and f—'

'Mr Armstrong!'

'Sorry. No, of course I didn't steal the—'

'And you know nothing about the disappearance of Mr Dixon?'

'No! I'm a fu—'

Linda merely raised a finger at this threatened obscenity.

'Fun-loving librarian,' said Israel.

'Well, you understand that I had to ask.'

'Oh, yes. That's fine, you and everyone else assuming I did it because I'm—'

'I was simply asking, Mr Armstrong.'

'Yes, sure. Because you're Perry bloody Mason, aren't you?'

'I beg your—'

'You know, Linda, I have spent all morning with—'

'What did you say?'

'I was saying, I have spent all morning—'

'No. Before that.'

'What?'

'You said I was like Perry bloody Mason.'

'Well, yes, I—'

'I resent the implication, Mr Armstrong.'

'What implication?' said Israel.

'Clearly, I am not a man,' said Linda.

'No one said you were a man, Linda.'

'And I am certainly not a bearded man.'

'I didn't say you were a bearded man.'

'Or an overweight bearded man.'

'Linda, come on, it was a—'

'Joke?'

'Exactly.'

'Well, I'm afraid many of us here don't seem to share your fancy London sense of humour, Mr Armstrong.'

'No. That's right,' said Israel. 'You don't. Because everyone in this bloody country has had a sense of humour bypass.'

'Thank you, Mr Armstrong. Less of your racial stereotyping would be appreciated,' said Linda. 'But anyway.' She took another – unconvinced – sip of her herbal tea, and fixed Israel with a stare. 'I'm afraid given the seriousness of the charges we're going to have to suspend you from your duties.'

Israel was having trouble following Linda's logic: he wasn't guilty of anything, after all.

'But—'

'With immediate effect,' said Linda.

'From now?'

'That's correct. That's why I've had to call you in today. That's what immediate effect usually means *over here*, Mr Armstrong, in this *bloody* country. I don't know if it carries a different meaning over in England's green and pleasant land?'

'No. It doesn't. It means the same.'

'Well then.'

'Suspended with immediate effect.'

Linda waved a finger at him, in dismissal.

'But—'

'There's nothing I can do about it, Mr Armstrong, I'm afraid.'

'But I haven't done anything wrong. I was in the wrong place at the wrong time.'

'Well, I believe you obviously. I hardly think you'd be capable of pulling off a daring and audacious robbery.'

'Thank you.'

'You're welcome. But, I doubt the Mobile Library Steering Committee will be of the same opinion I'm afraid. So . . .'

Linda made for the door.

'Hang on,' said Israel. 'That's it?'

'Yes,' said Linda. 'That's it. Thank you, goodbye.'

'Hang on! Who's going to be doing the mobile?'

'Ted. He'll be doing it on his own for the moment, when he can, although we'll have to be operating a reduced service, obviously.'

'But . . .'

'Ah, yes!' said Linda. 'Which brings me to the third thing. Point three. Before you leave, please.' She walked back behind her desk and sat down. 'Sit down. Please,' she said. 'Sit down! Thank you. Yes. About your lovely assistant on the library.'

'Ted?'

'No. Not Ted! Rosie.'

'Rosie?'

'Rosie Hart has been helping you out, I believe, in the fulfilment of your duties.'

'Yes. That's right. She's very good with the readers.'

'Yes.' Linda sipped at her tea. 'I'm sure that's not the only thing she's good with.'

'What?'

'With your reputation, Mr Armstrong, you need to be very careful.'

'My reputation?'

'Yes. We've not forgotten your dealings with the gutter press, Mr Armstrong—'

'If you mean by that my . . . friendship with Veronica Byrd of the *Impartial Recorder*—'

'Not something we wish to go into, Mr Armstrong. Has Ms Hart been offering her services to you for free?'

'Her services?'

'On the mobile library? Has she been working for you for free?'

'Not exactly.'

'So you've been paying her yourself?'

'Well . . . I've been . . .'

'Yes?' Linda peered over the top of her glasses.

'Erm. Yes, using the petty cash to . . .'

'Yes?'

'Give her a few pounds. Just to help her out, you know.'

'I see. This is what we'd heard. So you have been using the monies of the Department of Entertainment, Leisure and Community Services to pay for an extra member of staff. Do you deny it?'

'No, not exactly.'

'With no authorisation.'

'Erm . . .'

'Or agreement. With no advertisement. No Equal Opportunities monitoring.'

'Well—'

'Which is in itself an extremely grave matter, Mr Armstrong, as I'm sure you can appreciate, never mind your unfortunate position vis-à-vis the robbery and kidnapping.'

'I don't have an unfortunate position vis-à-vis the robbery and kidnapping!'

'We want her off the bus, Mr Armstrong.'

'But—'

'Thank you. And I'm afraid during your suspension you will have to attend a disciplinary hearing of the Mobile Library Steering Committee.'

'But—'

'You are going to have to learn, Mr Armstrong, that you can't just come over here and start playing fast and loose: there are rules here, you know, same as anywhere else. It's not a free-for-all.'

Linda once more made for the door, but then paused.

'Keys, please.' She held out her hand. 'For the van.'

'I can't give you the keys,' said Israel.

'Keys.'

'But I'll be stranded without the van.'

'Well, you should have thought of that before—'

'Linda, it's still at Dixon and—'

'We'll collect it. Thank you. Goodbye.' She was holding open the door.

'This is ridiculous, Linda,' said Israel. 'I have been unjustly accused of a crime I did not commit. This is a civil liberties issue.'

Linda laughed – and a wave of hot peppermint tea fumes came over Israel.

'You're hardly Nelson Mandela, Mr Armstrong.'

'I didn't say I was Nelson bloody Mandela, did I.'

'Racist remarks of any kind, Mr Armstrong, are a serious disciplinary offence, and I have already had to warn you about this today.'

'I wasn't making a—'

'Nelson Mandela was the father of a nation.'

'Yes. I know.'

'Which is not a category you find yourself in, unless I'm much mistaken.'

'No. I didn't—'

'Unless you do have anything of any substance to add, I think that'll be all. Keys. Please.'

'I haven't got the keys, the police have got the keys.'

'Very good,' said Linda. 'Thank you, Mr Armstrong. You'll be hearing from me about the disciplinary committee. Goodbye!'

And with that she was gone.

Ted was waiting for Israel outside the council offices, smoking.

'Well?'

'I'm suspended,' said Israel, hurrying after him.

'Aye,' said Ted. 'That'd be about right. On full pay though?'

'I don't know. I didn't ask.'

'Ach, are you soft in the head, man? Ye didnae ask?'

'I didn't think.'

'No. Did it go all right though?'

'No,' said Israel. 'It didn't go all right. And Linda seemed a bit . . .'

'Aye. Ye not heard? Her husband's away.'

'What, gone?'

'Aye. Left her. And they've five weans.'

'That's terrible.'

'Mind,' said Ted, lowering his voice. 'People say she's a Libyan.'

'What? I thought she was Northern Irish Chinese,' said Israel.

'No, a Libyan, you know,' said Ted, winking.

'A Libyan? You've lost me, Ted, I'm afraid.'

'She's not as other women are,' said Ted.

'A lesbian?' said Israel.

'Sshh,' said Ted. 'We'll not have that sort of language round here, thank ye.'

They got back in Ted's cab.

'So now what?' said Ted.

'I don't know,' said Israel.

'We're just going to have to clear yer name, aren't we?' said Ted.

'We?' said Israel.

'Aye,' said Ted. 'You're going to need some help with this, aren't ye?'

'Well, it's very nice of you and everything, but—'

'What?'

'I think I'm going to have to handle this one on my own, Ted.'

'Handle it on your own?' Ted laughed.

'What's funny?'

'You're a geg, you know that?'

'Am I?'

'How ye going to handle it then?'

'Well, I just need to work it out and demonstrate to the police that—'

'This is the PSNI we're talking about here, ye know?'

'Yes.'

'And what, ye think you're going to prove your innocence to them by using your powers of superior intelligence? Present them with a wee dossier setting out what a good little boy ye are?'

'Well . . .'

'Ach, you're better value than watching the telly, d'you know that?'

'Thank you.'

'Priceless, honestly. So, what, ye'll get back to me when you need me then, eh?' Ted was chuckling.

'Sure.'

Ted checked his watch. 'That'll be tomorrow teatime then, I would have thought.'

'Ha, ha.'

'No. Afternoon. At the latest.'

'Fine, Ted. If you could just take me home, please. I'm really—'

'Midday, we'll say. Half twelve max,' said Ted.

'Fine. Ted—'

'You've got my mobile number?'

'Yes.'

'If You Want To Get There, Call the Bear.'

'Sure. I'll keep you informed.'

'You'll keep *me* informed?'

'Yeah.'

'Brilliant. Priceless. I'm looking forward to this.'

CHAPTER 7

Ted dropped Israel back at the Devines' in his cab.

When he walked into the farmyard Israel noticed a big pile of things outside the door of the chicken coop – which was his home, howsoever so humble. The bird has its nest, and the fox its hole, and Israel had . . . well, he'd got used to it.

As he approached closer he saw that the pile of things outside the door of the coop was in fact a pile of his *own* things from *inside* the coop, which didn't look good.

Indeed, as he approached closer still he saw that the pile was a pile of *all* his things from inside the coop: his suitcase, his clothes, his books, everything, cast out and dumped, a big spew of stuff, like damp kindling for a bonfire.

The door of the coop was open. He stepped inside.

There was nothing there. It was empty – his home, stripped bare. The bed had gone. The old rag rugs had gone. The little Baby Belling had gone. Only the old sink with its single cold tap, nailed to the wall with battens, indicated that the chicken coop might ever have been fit for human habitation.

Israel took a deep breath. He told himself that this was only to be expected, frankly, on a day like today, and he could take it, no problem; one more thing was not going to tip him over the edge – because he'd been way over the edge already, several times – and he walked calmly across to the farmhouse, into the kitchen, looking for someone to grab a hold of and to throttle, George ideally, but really anyone would do. And of course it was old Mr Devine who was there because he was always there, like the Rayburn and the smell of stewed tea.

As far as Israel could recall he'd never seen Mr Devine anywhere else but in the kitchen at the farm; it was possible he even slept there, on the big rush-seated chair by the range, pot of tea just a reach away, and the milk jug covered by the little net with beads hanging from it, just like Israel's grandmother used to have. He was a permanent fixture.

He couldn't throttle Mr Devine, alas: that'd be bad luck. Mr Devine was like a household god, a little toothless talisman, always to be relied upon, bundled up in his chair reading the paper or a magazine, or standing ironing furiously, as if by ironing he could be rid of all the wrinkles in the world. Today he was sitting, reading a magazine, squinting at it right up close. He didn't much approve of books, Mr Devine, apart from the Bible, but magazines were OK, it seemed; magazines had less in them, so were less likely to lead us into temptation and he always had two or three on the go at the same time. The *People's Friend* he liked very much, and *Ireland's Own*. Today he was reading *Fancy Fowl*, his favourite chicken magazine.

Israel took another deep breath to calm himself: he could cope with this.

There was a strong smell in the kitchen, as there always was, the smell of tea and stewed meat, a dense thicket of smell, as if something were coming up out of the ground, a smell so strong, so primeval it was enough to make you dizzy just walking in there; it was like inhaling earth, or ingesting a big bowl of mutton- and beef-rich stew. Israel hadn't yet got round to telling the Devines he was a vegetarian and he could think of no easy way to explain it now; as so often for Israel the moment seemed to have passed, and he'd missed the boat, and that was it, he was stuck. He ate mostly by himself in his coop, but sometimes he ended up eating with George and Mr Devine, if Brownie was home from university, and he'd always just pretend he wasn't hungry, although of course he was hungry; he was hungry all the time; he was hungry now, for example, and the smell of the meat seemed to call out deeply to him. He swallowed hard.

'Mr Devine?' said Israel.

'Hmm,' said Mr Devine, without looking up from *Fancy Fowl*. 'The fish vomited out Jonah upon dry land.'

'Sorry?'

'We thought you was in the hands of the law.'

'Erm. Yes. I was, but I'm out now. And my . . . Erm. All my things seem to be out in the yard.'

'Aye. That's right.'

'Well, I was, you know, wondering why?'

'The PSNI was in here, asking after you.'

'Oh.'

'Blessed is the man that walketh not in the counsel of the ungodly.'

'Yes. Right. What did they want, the police?'

'You'll have us scandalled all the way to the border.'

'Sorry. Yes. Erm. What did they want?'

'You'd have to be speaking to George about that.'

'OK. It's the bed as well, you see, my bed in the coop, it's gone.'

'Gideon lay down a fleece to see if it was God's will that he were to save Israel.'

'Right. OK. The bed and the furniture, though?'

'Book of Judges.'

'Right. The bed – it's not there any more.'

'Aye, well. Like I say, you'd have to be speaking to George about it.'

'OK. Fine. And George is?'

Mr Devine glanced at the greasy-faced clock on the mantelpiece above the Rayburn. 'She'd be up in Toagher.'

'What, sorry? Where?'

'Toagher,' said Mr Devine.

'Right,' said Israel.

Toagher was of course Two Acre in Israel's standard north London English. It was a field. They had all these names for the fields round the farm and Israel could never remember what they were, or where they were, or how you were supposed to tell the difference between them – a field looked like a field to him, plus or minus hedges, and minus mostly. I mean, how the hell were you supposed to tell the difference between, say, the Well Field and the Stile Field, neither of which had an actual well or a stile in them any more, but which had done, apparently, forty or fifty years previously, when old Mr Devine was a young man and the names had been handed down from whiskery old men who had survived into their nineties on nothing more than floury potatoes, strong pipe tobacco, a few whelks and some seaweed? A lot of the fields were named after people, the fathers and grandfathers of the old whiskery ones, not because they looked like the people, which might have been a clue because frankly round here most people had pre-industrial topographic features, but because there was some ancient obscure kinship tie. And then there were the Four Wee Fields, which was in fact only one field; and the Wee Back Field, which was only at the back if you could remember that the back of the farm used to be the front and the front the back, which wasn't entirely clear to the newcomer.

'Just remind me, where's Two Acre?'

'Yon by the Black Field.'

'OK, great. Super.'

The Black Field. The Black Field was so called because there was something obscurely bad about it, but unless you'd lived round about for two or three centuries the libel left you cold; how the hell were you supposed to know which was the Black bloody Field?

'Thank you. I'll go and . . .'

'When Gideon died the children of Israel forsook God and worshipped Baal.'

'Well, I'm sorry to hear that. I have to . . .' Israel made for the door.

'And your mother rang,' called Mr Devine.

'Sorry?'

'Your mother.'

'Really?' Israel's mother never rang. 'Here?'

'Aye.'

'You didn't mention to her that the police were here, did you?'

'Aye.'

'Right. Is that an "Aye, yes", or an "Aye, no"?'

'Aye.'

'Right.' Two ayes, in Israel's experience in and around Tumdrum, usually meant a yes. 'Oh, God.'

'Thou shalt not take the name of the Lord thy God in vain; for the Lord will not hold him guiltless that taketh his name in vain.'

100

'Yes. Sorry. Forgot. Did she say what she wanted at all?'

'Who?'

'My mother?'

'Aye.'

'Right . . .'

'She said can you ring her.'

'OK. Did it sound urgent?'

'Aye.'

'I'll take that as a yes, then, shall I?'

Israel's mother had pretty much given up ringing him now that he was here; in fact since he'd moved to Northern Ireland his mother seemed to have given up on him entirely. She'd never approved of him becoming a librarian in the first place. She was a snob, his mother, that was her trouble; in her mind, a librarian was somewhere on the social scale just below social worker and just above bus driver; indeed, she could barely utter the word 'librarian'. When people asked, she used to tell them that Israel worked in 'information services'. She thought it sounded better, which, to be honest, it did. She'd hoped of course that he'd have turned out as a doctor, with maybe a law degree up his sleeve in case of emergencies, so for him to have turned out as a librarian – an 'information manager' – a mere purveyor of books, that was bad enough, but to be a librarian on a mobile library in Northern Ireland . . . *'Oy ve!'* she might have cried, throwing her hands up in the air, because she often did exactly that, just like the people of Northern Ireland, in Israel's experience, often said 'Ach' and 'Aye' and 'But' at the end of their sentences, and viewed you with narrowed eyes and hunched shoulders. But if you were to write that down and describe it thus no one would believe you; they'd think you were exaggerating, or making things up. People thought they were unique, and that they lived lives of utter complexity and singularity, that they were free and unfettered to be and do and act however and whatever they willed, but in Israel's experience it was otherwise: in his experience, people lived lives entirely bound by their limited background and circumstances. Librarians were just so much like librarians, and his mother was Jewish, and the problem with people in Northern Ireland was that they were so Northern Irish. And his problem? Israel's problem was that he was a Jewish librarian living in Northern Ireland.

If his mother was ringing then it must be important. Israel wondered if maybe she'd won the National Lottery; she'd been doing the same numbers now for years. She seemed to believe that the Lottery was like a queue for a fairground attraction, that it was only a matter of time before it was her turn to step up and get a go and claim her prize, and preferably in a Euro rollover week.

Israel used the phone in the front room, down beneath the photos of the Loyal Orange Lodge; the police had his mobile, and his *London Review of Books*, and his lint.

Israel had never exactly been good on the phone, and he was getting worse. His calls to Gloria these days were an absolute disaster. They used to have good phone days and bad phone days, but now they'd pretty much given up on actually talking to each other. When he first arrived Israel used to leave messages on the home phone, back at the flat they'd shared together, but it was always on answerphone, and the sound of Gloria's voice – that low, direct tone she'd use whenever she wanted something done, or when she wanted to sound in charge: 'I'm not here right now, but if you leave a message I'll get back to you' – that was too much for him. So they'd turned instead to texting. Or at least Israel had turned to texting. Gloria had bought him *The Lt Bk of Txt* last Christmas – as well as a nice Thomas Pink tie, he should add, and some CDs – and he'd really taken to it. It was a bit like writing, only easier. The problem was, the texting had turned into a one-way correspondence.

'LO,' he'd text.

No reply.

'LO?'

No reply.

'RUOK?'

No reply.

'RUF2T?'

No reply.

'PCM.'

No reply.

'PLS.'

No reply.

The most she'd ever text back would be: 'SPK.'

But they rarely did.

But that was OK. They were going to sort everything out. Gloria was coming over next weekend and Israel was planning to take her round and show her the sights, and he was going to get Ted to help him work out an itinerary. And of course he'd have sorted out all this nonsense with the police and everything would be fine, fine, fine. Things would get back to normal. They were going to have a great time.

His mum picked up.

'Hi, Mum,' he said.

'Hello?'

'It's me.'

'Who's me?'

'Your son, Israel.'

'Ah,' said his mum.

She hadn't won the National Lottery. She'd rung Israel at the farm to tell him that his grandmother – Granny G they called her – had gone into hospital.

Granny G had been ill for a long time. She was Israel's last surviving grandparent. The others had died when he was much younger – one cancer, one heart attack, one stroke, the usual dull, limited range of diseases. Israel had always wished they could have died of something more interesting and exotic. Gloria's grandfather had died of a tropical disease he'd picked up in Africa, but then Gloria's family were exactly that sort of family; Israel's family were more the sort that died of complications arising from a fall in the bathroom, or a hospital infection from a wound after surgery.

Israel's granny had been ill almost as long as Israel remembered her. It was her hips when he was in his teens and then there was the angina, and recently she'd been getting out of breath. He hadn't been able to keep up with her illnesses when he was living at home – they'd all started to merge into one – and there was no way he'd been able to keep up with them now, from a distance. Listening to someone describing someone else's sicknesses on the phone acted like a sedative on Israel.

But this was different. His mother really sounded worried. She'd been coughing a lot, apparently, Granny G, had lost a lot of weight and now she was in for tests. Bronchoscopy, was it his mother said? Israel told his mother not to worry, he was sure she'd be fine. She'd always recovered before; she'd recover this time too.

'And what's this about the police?' said his mother.

'What?'

'The police? The old man on the phone there said something about—'

'Sorry, Mum, it's a bad line. I can't hear you properly . . .'

'The police!' said his mother. 'You're in trouble?'

'Mum, sorry. I'll have to call you back some-time. OK. Thanks, bye.'

When he returned to the kitchen George was there. She was wearing her faded blue boiler suit and her hair was pinned up; she looked as though she might have been out fixing up Formula I racing cars.

'Armstrong,' she said.

'Ah, yes, George,' said Israel. 'My belong-ings . . .'

'Yes?'

'They were out in the yard.'

'Yes.'

'And that's because?'

'The police were here, Armstrong.'

'Yes. I'm sorry about that. I seem to have got mixed up in this—'

'They told us,' said George. 'They wanted your passport.'

'Right.'

'Did you do it?' she asked.

George had folded her arms; she often folded her arms when speaking to him, purposefully and resentfully, as though Israel had made her do it, as though he himself had imposed the burden upon her, as if he'd said, 'Fold your arms, woman!' It was a gesture that suggested scepticism and annoyance and boredom and above all contempt; with a mere movement of hand to elbow George knew how to blow a chill wind into a room and through a conversation.

'Did you do it?' she repeated, arms firmly in place.

'Well!' said Israel indignantly. He'd have done an '*Oy ve!*' if he thought he could've got away with it, but what was the point of an exclamation if no one knew what it meant? Since moving to Northern Ireland he'd had to give up about half his repertoire of verbal and non-verbal exclamations; he'd had to adapt; his hands, his mouth, his entire body had had to accommodate themselves to the landscape and to the people.

'Well!' he said again, folding his arms in imitation of George. 'Did I do it? Oh, yes. Oh, yes. Silly me.' He slapped his forehead. 'I almost forgot! Of course I did it! I stole all the money from the department store, kidnapped Mr Dixon, and now I'm hiding him until I get paid the ransom. You caught me fair and square. I'm your man. It's a fair cop.'

'Joy shall there be in heaven over one sinner that repenteth,' said Mr Devine, scratching his grizzly chin.

'So,' said George, arms still folded.

'Of course I didn't do it!' said Israel. 'What do you think I am? I'm a librarian. I'm not a bloody criminal!'

'Aye, well. We don't actually know anything about you, Mr Armstrong. You could well be a librarian *and* a bloody criminal for all we're to know.'

'We'll not have language in the house,' said Mr Devine.

'All right, Grandad,' said George. 'Sorry.'

'Parcel of bad meat,' muttered Mr Devine.

'What?' said Israel.

'You are an unknown quantity,' said George.

'Right. Yes. Of course. Well, there you are. Sorry. You've found me out. Truth is, I'm not the mild-mannered fellow I seem. I'm a dangerous criminal on the run from Interpol. Wanted across Europe for a string of department store crimes.'

'There's no need for your sarcasm, Mr Armstrong,' said George.

'Well, honestly. Who do you think I am?'

George looked at him sternly and Israel decided to try a subtler, more sympathetic approach to George's wall of discontent.

'Look. OK. Listen. This . . . thing will all be sorted out in a couple of days. OK? And you'll see I have nothing *whatsoever* to do with it, and that'll be us, back to the way we were. All right?' Israel looked pleadingly from George to Mr Devine. 'So can I put my stuff back in the coop?'

'No, Armstrong,' said George. 'We need the chicken coop.'

'What do you mean you need the chicken coop? What for?'

'For chickens.'

'But you didn't need it this morning!'

'Things have changed since this morning, Mr Armstrong.'

'But you can't have the coop for chickens.'

'Chickens need to be inside,' said George.

108

'But that's where I live!' said Israel.

'Was,' said George. 'And just to remind you, you've been complaining and threatening—'

'Threatening?' said Israel.

'Complaining and *promising*,' said George. 'Promising to find somewhere else to live since you first arrived here.'

'Yes. Well, I haven't managed to sort it out yet. I've had a lot to . . . And you can't just throw me out on the street.'

'No.'

'No, you can't! I'm paying you good money to put me up.'

'Yes. You are.'

'Well then.'

'We're not throwing you out,' said George.

'But you just said . . .'

'We've decided you can stay in Brownie's room while he's away at university.'

'Oh, right.'

That came as a surprise. That sounded quite good. It was actually in the house.

'Actually in the house?' said Israel.

'We can keep a closer eye on you there.'

'Ah, right. Well. That's . . . Well. That's very good. So where's Gloria going to stay?'

'Who?'

'My girlfriend, Gloria? She's coming over next weekend. I told you. You know all about that. Don't pretend you don't know.'

'She certainly can't stay here, Armstrong.'

'Why not?'

'You're not married, are you?'

'No.'

'Well, you're not cohabiting here then.'

Mr Devine shook his head in agreement.

'But—'

'We'll be charging you extra, mind,' said George.

'What?'

'For the inside of the house.'

'Oh, good grief.'

'Is that a problem, Armstrong?'

'No, no, not at all. In fact, I'll tell you what, how about I give you all my wages at the end of every month and you just pay me a small allowance and keep the rest?'

'Have you seen the price of pig feed recently?' asked George.

'Erm. No,' said Israel.

'And the permits and th'pig passports,' added Mr Devine.

'Pig passports?'

'Aye.'

'Bird flu. All we need now is swine fever, and that'd be us,' said Mr Devine.

'Don't talk like that, Granda,' said George.

'Sorry?' said Israel.

'You remember the fire at Lovell and Christmas a few years back?' said Mr Devine.

'No.'

'All them Large Whites.'

'Are they potatoes?' said Israel.

'They're pigs, for goodness sake,' said George.

'Oh, right. Sorry.'

'Anyway,' said George.

'We're losing money on every one,' said Mr Devine.

'If you're in Brownie's room you're responsible for the fish,' said George.

'What? This is a fish farm as well? What is it, salmon or trout?'

'They're tropical fish,' said George.

'Ah,' said Israel.

'In Brownie's aquarium.'

Israel spent the rest of the afternoon shifting his things from the yard into Brownie's room, which was pretty much what you'd expect of a young man's room: the obligatory Kurt Cobain poster; some wrestling posters, featuring men who looked like they'd been dipped in body-building plastic; and piles of books on the obligatory wobbly shelves, full of textbooks, a copy of *The Dice Man*, and J.K. Rowlings. There was also an accordion, which Israel picked up and gave a good squeeze – he'd got up to Grade 5 piano, after all, and he managed to get a couple of chords out of it – and then there was the *pièce de résistance*, the aquarium. Brownie had gone for the traditional treasure chests, divers and mermaids; and fish, of course. George had given him the guided tour.

'That's a Veiltail Betta.'

'Right.'

'And that's an African Jewel Fish.'

'OK.'

'Paradise Fish.'

'Uh-huh.'

'Dwarf Gourami.'

'Hello, Mr Gourami!' said Israel, waving at the fish.

'They're fish, Armstrong.'

'Yes, right, just sort of—'

'And that's a Red-breasted Cichlid.'

'Good.'

'Brownie loves his fish,' said George.

'Well, perfect pet,' said Israel. 'Much better than dogs or cats.'

George looked at him askance.

'Not that I don't like cats and dogs,' he added quickly; there were several cats on the farm, and a black Labrador that padded here and there that the Devines referred to simply as the Gundog. Israel had never liked dogs, or cats. Gloria wanted a cat. But cats scratched.

'Hemingway kept cats,' he said, catching sight of Brownie's copy of *A Farewell to Arms*.

'I'm sure. Whatever you do, don't forget to feed the fish,' said George.

'I won't,' said Israel. 'I shall treat them as my own.'

The aquarium was tucked up under the window, from where you got to see the farm in all its squalor and glory. Framed in the distance, right in the centre of the window – rotten wooden sash windows, the cords frayed – there was the old oak, up past the New Field, with some sort of an over-grown shrubbery around it; and then off to the left, closer to the house, the long low buildings where they kept the pigs, with the yard and the barns, covered with Virginia creeper and ivy; and then the disused well off to the right with its old wooden cover, like some passageway down to the centre of the earth; and Mr Devine's vegetable patch, with its rows and rows of leeks and onions. Smooth, hazy hills curved downwards to meet this view, the farm a mere foreground to vast, unrolling, magnificent nature.

You couldn't deny that kind of view; there was no getting round it, no going under it: it was idyllic. Sometimes – and it had happened more than once now, though he didn't like to admit it – Israel thought this might be a good place to live.

But then he'd remember he was actually living here.

By the time he'd finished unpacking his things it was after dark and Israel lay down on Brownie's bed to read.

Brownie had a shelf of crime paperbacks next to the aquarium – slightly damp crime paperbacks – and Israel had started flicking through them, in the hope that the books might help him in some way, that they might have the answer to all his problems. He'd never read a lot of crime fiction before; it was the covers, mostly, that put him off. He was very anti-embossing.

He lay on the bed for hours, entranced, flicking

through tales of absurd and horrific murders solved in the most improbable fashion. He'd pick up a book and start reading it, and he'd get to where the hero, the detective, or the forensic pathologist, or the maverick investigator, was hot on the trail of the mobsters, or the serial killer, or the corrupt businessman who nobody suspected, and they were also having to face up to some demons of their own – drink, usually, or a troublesome ex-husband or wife – and then he'd realise that the whole thing was just ridiculous and getting him nowhere, and he'd toss the book aside and take up another. It was like eating a family pack of Tayto cheese and onion crisps (which he'd done, actually, several times, so he knew).

By about midnight he was satiated and utterly, utterly depressed; his eyes ached and his head hurt, and also he was starving. Judging by the books he was reading he was going to need a car, and probably a gun in order to get anywhere in his investigation; it would also help if he had a complex inner life and a troubled childhood. But first he needed something to eat.

So he crept downstairs to the kitchen.

There were no lights on anywhere. Israel felt around trying to find them, but failed; he'd never been inside the house by himself at night. He felt his way to where he thought the fridge might be, and knelt down, opened the door, felt the cold and the light upon him, and began looking for what he could find: some lard, some dripping,

114

some hard cheese, and lots of uncooked meat – sausages, mostly, and bacon. But then also, wrapped in foil, he found the remains of the Devines' dinner: a chicken carcass.

Now this was a serious dilemma.

Israel hadn't eaten meat since he was eighteen years old, although he'd thought about it probably every day since, and he looked at the pale stringy flesh hanging from the bones and couldn't decide – it looked so pathetic – but then he remembered those nuggety little bits of meat that you get under the chicken, those little goujons, and he turned the chicken over and there they were, white and glistening in the fridge's glow. He was just prising them off and was about to pop them in his mouth when someone kicked open the kitchen door and yelled at him, 'You move and I'll kill you!'

He leapt up and put his hands in the air.

George was at the doorway in a tartan dressing gown, with a shotgun.

'Jesus Christ!' said Israel, still with his hands up.

'Armstrong!'

'George!'

'What in God's name are you doing in here?'

'I live here,' said Israel.

'Not in the kitchen!'

'No. I was just—'

'You can put your hands down,' said George.

'Right. Thanks.' Israel had the little chicken bits in the palms of his hands. 'Erm . . .'

'You're lucky I didn't . . .'

'Quite,' said Israel.

'You ragin' eejit,' said George.

'Sorry. That's the second time today someone's pointed a gun at me, actually.'

'Aye, well, maybe third time lucky,' said George, lowering the gun.

'Right. Thanks,' said Israel.

George was turning to go.

'Actually, George,' said Israel.

'What?'

'I need to ask you a favour.'

'No,' said George, turning back.

'Please. You haven't heard what it is yet.'

'No. It's midnight. You're in my kitchen stealing my food, and you're lucky you're not bleedin' like a stuck pig. So the answer to whatever you're asking is no.'

'It's just . . .'

'*No!* Do you understand the word?'

'Yes. It's just, I just wondered about your . . . erm, your gun there? If I could maybe borrow it if I needed it?'

'Are you out of your tiny English mind, Armstrong?'

'No. It's just—'

'No! *No! No!*'

'What about the car then? Could I maybe borrow the car tomorrow? Just while I've not got the van to fall back on.'

'No!'

'But I need some transport, George, at least, if I'm going to be able to prove my innocence, and I've only got a week to—'

'It's not my problem, Armstrong. You've got yourself into a mess, you get yourself out of it. *Without* my gun, and *without* my car – you lunatic! Goodnight,' she said, slamming the door behind her.

'Goodnight,' said Israel feebly.

He looked at the chicken pieces in his hand, and put them in the bin. He'd lost his appetite.

If he'd been a detective in one of Brownie's crime novels he'd have drunk a half-bottle of whisky and gone driving off into the night listening to his favourite music while making incredible deductive leaps.

Instead, he felt silently sorry for himself, made a cup of tea and went to bed.

CHAPTER 8

The Reverend England Roberts stood at the front of the church. He was wearing his customary grey lounge suit and his far too wide, Adam's-apple-accentuating dog collar, and he was speaking – or, rather, booming – in his usual fashion into a microphone, which seemed to distort and amplify not merely his words, but also his personality. His habitual mischievous gleaming smile had been replaced with that peculiar look of the Christian ministering, that look that Israel had seen on the faces of all the old Presbyterian ministers in the photographs in the Reverend Roberts's robing room, a look way beyond smiling, a look of perfect yet somehow undefined profundity, a look of brow-furrowing tranquillity, as though contemplating some utterly obvious yet infinitely complex mathematical problem. It was a look . . . Israel was trying to think where he'd seen that look before. Well, to be honest, it was a post-coital kind of a look, that was what it was, Israel thought, though it seemed wrong, confusing sexual and religious emotions, particularly in a church, mixing up ultimate and penultimate truths. He had to shake his head to get the thought out of his mind; but then that was religion for you, in his opinion: it got you all confused.

The reverend was reading from the tiny brown leather pocket Bible in his hand.

'"Early on the Sunday morning,"' he boomed, the church's loudspeakers rattling its vast accompaniment of hums and whistles, '"while it was still dark, Mary of Magdala came to the tomb."' The deep 'oo' of the reverend's 'tomb' here rang high and low, reverberating around the church, setting off a high-pitched feedback to follow it, which came bouncing off the walls like some small demented creature hurtling in pursuit of a big bass-baritone bear. As the reverend took a breath and paused between intonations, a man wearing a canary-yellow tie and an ill-fitting brown polyester suit that crackled as he moved darted forward from the front row of seats, and started fiddling with the cable of the microphone. The Reverend Roberts paused until the man in the suit gave a thumbs up, nodded apologetically and retreated back, statically, from whence he had come.

'OK. Thank you. Is that better?' asked England, booming clearly now without feedback or echo. The congregation nodded silent assent. 'OK. Good. Good. Now' – the reverend waved a hand towards heaven but addressed the congregation – 'Brothers and sisters' – and Israel felt a little shudder go through the congregation at that; he guessed they weren't accustomed to being addressed as such – 'Brothers and sisters,' repeated the reverend, unrepentant, 'I want you to imagine that you were there on that morning. Can you imagine that? Can you imagine that you *were* Mary, going to the tomb? Can you imagine what that might have been like for a young woman going to see her Lord? The man she had seen crucified and died, just days – not even days, just hours – earlier. And now there she is *in the dark* we are told – which is a *wonderful* image. In the dark, both *literally* and metaphorically.'

Israel glanced around him nervously. The congregation was rapt. He was sitting towards the back: he bent down and removed his bicycle clips.

Israel had not been able to persuade George to let him have the use of the car in order to conduct his investigation into the theft of the money from Dixon and Pickering's and Mr Dixon's mysterious disappearance, but George had very generously allowed him to use Brownie's old bike, a Raleigh Elswick Hopper with Sturmey Archer three-speed gears, and a wicker basket up front. So at least he had a means of transport to be able to set about clearing his name, though he had no idea, frankly, exactly how a man might set out to do that; not usually by bike, he guessed.

His first decision was to go to church. He'd promised the Reverend Roberts months ago that he'd be there for the Easter morning service, and he felt he couldn't let him down, even under his current peculiar circumstances; also, to be honest, he was half hoping that in church he might receive some kind of divine guidance; it certainly couldn't be worse than stewing in his own considerable juices at the Devines', looking for an insight into how to solve a complex criminal investigation through the pages of Sue Grafton, Ian Rankin and George P. Pelecanos.

Israel hadn't ridden a bike since he was about ten years old and when he got on, he fell right off; there was either something wrong with the bicycle, or riding a bicycle is not like riding a bicycle: you do forget. He could remember his very first bike as a child: it was a candy-floss pink with multicoloured streamers attached to the handlebars and it had a squidgy purple seat; it had been handed down from one of his sisters. Israel had had to put up with a lot of hand-me-downs when he was young, which meant he'd become accustomed to girls' tastes in most things, including bicycles, and books, toys and music; Gloria thought that too many *Bunty* annuals and Madonna albums had maybe held Israel back in his career development and in his self-image and that he should perhaps go and get some counselling. According to Gloria, any man with a too developed fondness for Anne

121

Tyler and Barbara Trapido should really be trying to beef himself up in other areas; Gloria was very feminine herself, but she also did kung-fu. Israel had never really been the macho type: there was a little park near their house when they were growing up and his sisters would race round, doing laps on their bikes, and he was always happy in his given role as timekeeper; indeed, sometimes, looking back, he felt as if he was merely the observer of his own childhood rather than a full participant, like having off-peak membership at the gym.

'What about the brakes?' he'd said to George, pulling at the brakes on the bike that she'd grudgingly wheeled out of an outbuilding.

'Wee turn, she'll be right,' said George.

'I can't ride this,' he said.

'She's in need of some attention,' agreed George.

'Some attention? This bike doesn't need attention. This bike needs—'

'A wee bit of TLC.'

'Therapy,' said Israel. 'This bike has had a total nervous breakdown.'

It had ordinary raised handlebars with once white, now grey moulded hand grips, slide-pull calliper brakes with brake blocks as thin as cigarette paper, and black and white Raleigh Record 26 x $1^{3}/_{8}$ tyres bald as an old man in a cap in a park in winter. The old three-speed Sturmey Archer gears were encased in grease with a dodgy trigger control and the full-cover mudguards must once have been chrome but now were rust. The saddle was worn almost to the point of extinction.

'Does it go?' said George.

'Well, the wheels turn,' said Israel.

'That'll do you then,' said George, who promptly disappeared back into the farmhouse.

After a few tentative turns around the yard, Israel had left himself a good hour to make it into Tumdrum for the Easter service; the roads had been deserted and everything had gone smoothly until he'd come round the corner near the Four Road Ends, down there by Maureen Minty's kennels, cattery and pet cemetery, Animal Magic ('Caring For Pets From Cradle to Grave'). As he turned the corner another cyclist, who was coming at some speed in the other direction, and who'd clipped off the corner and was way over on the wrong side of the road, came hurtling towards him. Israel jammed on his brakes, which worked only under considerable pressure, and skidded to a halt, successfully avoiding the other cyclist, just as a little Peugeot driven by an old lady wearing a hat came cruising round from behind him at around 50 miles an hour and narrowly avoided killing them all.

The old lady sped on, keen to get to church, presumably, rather than get involved in any kind of road rage incident or insurance claim. Israel righted himself on the bike and prepared to start screaming at the other cyclist, who was wearing skin-tight leggings, a shiny silver helmet, wrap-around shades, and a bright blue cycling shirt with a zip front and back pockets.

'Armstrong!' called the cyclist, dismounting.

'Hello?' said Israel.

The cyclist flipped up his shades. It was Pearce Pyper.

'Good grief!' said Israel. 'It's you.'

'It is indeed!' said Pearce. 'Didn't know you cycled.'

'No. I didn't either,' said Israel. 'Not until this morning. I didn't know *you* cycled.'

'Ah. Hardly at all these days,' said Pearce, who was eighty if he was a day. 'Given it up. Do the odd one at the weekend, just to keep my hand in, you know.'

'Nice bike,' said Israel, admiring the black steel-framed cycle with its white lettering.

'Ah, yes. A De Selby. Italian. With Campag kit. Armstrong uses Shimano, you know.'

'Right.'

'But I prefer the Campag. More elegant.'

Another car came round the corner, from Pearce's direction this time, again driven by an old lady in a hat, and again narrowly missing them. Pearce raised his fist in anger as the car sped away.

'Shall we move?' said Israel, indicating the grass verge.

'Roadhogs,' said Pearce, hauling his bike to the side of the road. 'Do you shave your legs?' he asked.

'No, I don't,' said Israel.

'You'll have to shave your legs,' said Pearce.

'Right.'

'Aerodynamics. Not against your religion, is it?'

'No, I don't think so,' said Israel.

'My first wife, she wouldn't shave her legs. She was Jewish, did I say?' said Pearce.

'Yes. Yes, I think you did.'

'Strange woman. I'm all for the Mosaic laws, mind, when it comes to food. Perfectly sensible. You keep kosher?'

'No, I don't.'

'She was a great one for the pickles, my wife. Used to ship them over.'

'Good.'

'Anyway. Well done you!' said Pearce nonsensically. 'Good to see a young man out getting fit. The old transfer of atoms twixt man and machine.'

'Quite,' said Israel.

'More of it!' said Pearce, as he saddled up again and sped away.

It was always nice to bump into Pearce Pyper.

Israel cycled slowly and carefully the rest of the way and was delighted when he finally made it safely into Tumdrum and parked his bike outside the Baptist church.

The Baptist was one of the four churches in Tumdrum's main square. The churches sat one on each side of the square, like the Horsemen of the Apocalypse come to round up stragglers and put them in a pen: as well as the Baptist and the Reverend Roberts Presbyterian there were the Methodist and the Church of Ireland, and each of them were big, square, flat-fronted buildings, places that suggested that their original architects and builders, and possibly their current ministers and congregations too, might have erred theologically on the side of judgement rather than mercy. The churches of Tumdrum did not look like the churches Israel knew in England: there was no fancy brickwork, no stained glass, and no steeples; no hint of the Papish, or of the foolish temptations of this world. The architecture seemed to embody the ideas it expressed: if Protestantism was made of blocks and rendered concrete then this was probably what it would look like; architecturally you might describe the style as Armageddon Lite. The Presbyterians had a flagpole on the top of their building, which flew no flags, and the Methodists had nothing at all, except a poster advertising coffee mornings, and the traditional reminder that If God Seems Far Away, Then Guess Who's Moved? The Church of Ireland had a big stone stylised representation of some saint or other over the doorway, with a halo around his head, and as Israel was

126

not good on saints he had no idea who this was supposed to be: he had the usual beard and receding hairline, and what appeared to be a set of butter knives in his left hand and looked like a man who'd been ambushed, and was about to be shot by firing squad. Of all the churches in the centre of Tumdrum, if he had to pick, Israel would probably have gone for the Baptist; the Baptists had hanging baskets. Also, they were hosting the Reverend Roberts Easter Sunday ecumenical service.

'When I was growing up in South Africa,' continued the Reverend Roberts inside the church, 'back in Duduza, it was *really* possible at night to be in the dark, completely, for there to be no lights, none at all for as far as the eye could see, no light except for the light of the moon itself. And on a moonlit night my brothers and I would play outside with our friends, lit by the stars and by the constellations and the planets, more than any human eye can count, illuminated by the glories of the universe. *But* on a night when the clouds covered the moon, in that deep darkness we would stay together indoors, staying together for warmth, and also for comfort, to keep us from the dark and the threat of the dark. For the darkness of the night, that darkness is a profound darkness, a darkness that many of us know in our hearts. We know that darkness as the darkness of doubt, perhaps, or as the darkness of depression, of unforgiveness, of shame, and of grief.'

Israel shifted uncomfortably in his seat. He was thinking about *Heart of Darkness*. He'd done a post-colonial theory module in the last year of his degree and had never quite got to grips with it. It had let him down in his final mark; it had taken him most of the term just to read *Culture and Imperialism*.

'There are, I'm sure, many among us who will have had that exact same experience of Mary's,' continued the Reverend Roberts, 'of visiting the grave of a loved one, in desolation and in despair. We know – do we not? – we know what it is like to grieve. We know what it is like to have that heaviness in our hearts, to wish to be close to those whom we have loved, and who have loved us.'

Israel coughed and pushed his glasses up high onto his forehead. He had the beginnings of a headache. He wasn't accustomed to Christian services – the language, the clothes were completely alien to him. He'd been to a few Christian weddings, of course, but they'd all been sedate Church of England affairs, attended mostly by other people of his own age who didn't seem to have a clue what was going on either – including, sometimes, the bride and groom. At his friend John's wedding a few years back he'd been best man, but his only actual responsibility in the church had been to look smart and keep out of the way. So this was really a first for him, to be in the thick of it, in among the Protestant natives. The Reverend Roberts had invited him because it was ecumenical, he said, though Israel was unsure exactly how far Tumdrum's ecumenism extended: there were no Sikhs, for example, in the church, as far as he could tell, and no Orthodox Jews, Muslims, Hindus, Baha'i, or Zoroastrians either, if it's possible to tell a Zoroastrian from a distance, which it may not be; Israel's grasp of comparative religions was almost as shaky as his grasp on his own. Tumdrum's ecumenism seemed merely to extend to all elderly men, no matter which shade of brown, grey or black machine-washable suit they chose to wear, and to all elderly women, regardless of their style or colour of hat.

It was certainly quite a service: Israel had never experienced anything quite like it; it was difficult to tell whether it was a show, or a stand-up comedy routine, or a guided meditation; it seemed to be all of them at once, which was good value, if nothing else; and the ecumenical aspect meant that you got four vicars for the price of one. The service had begun with notices read out by one man in a dog collar – a nice old man with yellow teeth and a neatly trimmed beard – and then they'd sung a hymn, 'Amazing Grace', introduced by another man in a dog collar, though without a beard, and Israel was surprised to find that he knew both the tune and the words of the hymn: 'Through many dangers, toils and snares I have already come'.

Then some teenagers had done a little sketch about a man and a camel getting through the eye of a needle, which Israel couldn't follow at all; it was like something you'd expect from a troupe of French surrealists. And then there was another hymn, some soupy kind of a thing that he'd never heard of, followed by what was billed as a time of praise and worship, led by yet another man in a dog collar, a little fat man with a shiny face, during which segment of the show the congregation simply repeated the words 'Alleluia', 'How I love Him', 'Blessed Jesus', 'My Redeemer' and 'Jesus is Lord' dozens and dozens of times. At which point Israel had begun to speculate whether the Reverend Roberts was involved in some sort of weird cult.

'"She saw that the stone had been moved away from the entrance,"' continued the reverend, who'd been awarded the honour of the actual address; Israel wondered if all the vicars had drawn lots. The reverend was now roaming with the microphone at the front of the church, wandering up and down, holding the Bible lightly in his huge hands, like you might hold half of a limp sandwich, and he gestured dramatically behind him, to the front of the church, where there was a vast . . . thing. It was scenery: like something from an amateur dramatic production of *The Flintstones*. Someone had obviously spent a lot of time with a lot of cardboard, struts and supports and a lot of grey paint. The reverend was pointing to a vast cardboard/papier-mâché stone kind of a thing that was propped against a vast cardboard/papier-mâché tomb kind of a thing; which was at least ten foot wide by ten foot tall; just getting it into the church was nothing short of a miracle.

'"She saw that the stone had been moved away from the entrance, and ran to Simon Peter and the other disciple, the one whom Jesus loved." Note that,' said the reverend, '"The one whom Jesus loved". What was Jesus's meaning? What was His message? That was it. What did He show us? Love. Why did He go through this for us? For love.'

Israel was doing his best to concentrate on the reverend's story-telling and drama but he kept drifting off. He was thinking about Gloria. Did he love her? He did. He definitely did. They'd met in their last year at college; Gloria was an English student, just like him, and she was funny and smart, she drank pints and didn't mind just a bag of chips for dinner, and she'd read every book by Margaret Atwood, and so had he. They'd gone out together for years and eventually it had just seemed simpler and easier to move in together, so they did, and it was only then that their lives had started to go in different directions: Gloria's towards Sebastian Faulks, and a law conversion course and weekends in Paris and fancy restaurants, and Israel's towards the Discount Book Shop in the Lakeside

Shopping Centre in Thurrock in Essex. They'd changed. But they'd learned to compromise. Gloria's favourite film, for example – by far – was *Four Weddings and a Funeral*; his was Fellini's *La Strada*. So they'd learned to compromise on American mid-market drama and adventure at the cinema, and eventually Israel had found himself enjoying this junk, becoming addicted to it almost, savouring every last morsel of sugar-puffed dialogue and absurd plot twist and special effect. You can't always eat caviar; you couldn't watch Fellini every day.

'"They have taken the Lord out of his tomb, and we do not know where they have laid him,"' recited the Reverend Roberts. 'This is Mary, still lost in ignorance. Mary, who does not yet know God's secret wisdom, which is hidden from mankind, but which He had already chosen for our glory even before the world was made.'

Israel was now thinking about Pesach: they'd never really bothered with a seder meal at home; his mother had made half-hearted attempts to keep it going over the years, but none of them was really interested, and so they'd lost it, the four questions and the roasted egg dipped in salt water; all the rituals had been abandoned, and along with them about four thousand years of Jewish history; they exchanged Easter eggs instead. He remembered having an argument with his mother when he was in his early teens, a blazing row, and saying that he was happy to participate in her stupid meal as long as they didn't have to mention God, the Jewish people, or Israel, because he couldn't care less about any of them. His mother had gone as red as a beet borscht and sworn at him and raised her fists at him and called him a self-hating Jew. At the time he had no idea what that was; he'd had to ask his father, who was an atheist Catholic Irishman but an honorary Jew, just by virtue of having married Israel's mother, and his father had said that, as far as he understood it, the entire Bible was the unfolding story of self-hating Jews, and so Israel should take it as a compliment: 'Moses, St Paul, Sigmund Freud, Woody Allen,' said his dad. 'Relax! You're in good company!'

'"So Peter and the other set out and made their way to the tomb,"' continued the reverend. '"They were running side by side, but the other disciple outran Peter and reached the tomb first." They are racing to seek the truth about the Lord whom they love,' he glossed. 'They cannot wait. You will know, perhaps, the film *Chariots of Fire*, the story of the great athletes Eric Liddell and Harold Abrahams and their desire to run after the prize. "He peered in"' – and at this point the Reverend Roberts himself peered in behind the cardboard tomb – '"and saw the linen wrappings lying there, but did not enter."' The reverend lifted up what looked like bath towels from the floor.

'"Then Simon Peter came up, following him, and he went into the tomb." It doesn't tell us, brothers and sisters, but I believe that Simon Peter would have *rushed* into the tomb! I don't think he would have walked in! He would have run!'

The Reverend Roberts had one arm raised aloft.

Israel could sense the excitement among the congregation; the story seemed to be reaching its conclusion.

'"He saw the linen wrappings lying, and the napkin which had been over his head, not lying with the wrappings but rolled together in a place by itself." He knows that something's not right here. Something has gone wrong,' said the reverend, speaking quietly now.

'"Then the disciple who had reached the tomb first went in too" – he has plucked up the courage now, he is prepared – and he saw, "and believed" is what the Scriptures tell us, brothers and sisters. He *believed, instantly* that he had seen, "Until then they had not understood the scriptures, which showed that he must rise from the dead."'

'Now *this* is the message of Easter,' said the reverend, his voice rising. 'The empty tomb, my friends! This is the day that death died. This is the heart of the matter for us as believers, as Christians. If it is true – and we believe it is true – then we can be sure that God exists. With this, doubt vanishes! Through the resurrection Jesus demonstrates that He was who He proclaimed himself to be: the Way, the Truth, the Life. This is the very heart of what we believe.'

There was a quiet murmuring of assent from all around.

Israel was beginning to feel extremely uncomfortable.

The reverend had been standing in the mouth of the huge cardboard tomb as he spoke, and he then stepped back and pulled the papier-mâché boulder across the entrance.

There was silence for a moment in the church. Then, suddenly, the boulder rolled forward from the tomb's entrance, down a few steps and down the central aisle of the church, and the cardboard tomb started to topple forward and people in the congregation began to stand up in shock.

The man in the crackling polyester suit moved forward, but too late: the cardboard tomb fell down flat, making a noise like a stable door shutting.

'Holy fuck!' cried one shocked and unholy congregant, who was loudly and violently shushed, but who clearly expressed what everyone else was thinking.

For there at the front of the church was revealed: nothing.

The Reverend Roberts had disappeared.

Israel was stunned. He'd never seen anything like it in his life.

The organist kicked in with 'Now Let the Vault of Heaven Resound', and then there were final prayers, and the service came to an abrupt end, followed by an undignified rush towards tea, coffee and biscuits in the church hall out the back, where the Reverend Roberts had now miraculously reappeared and stood surrounded by old ladies in hats and men in grey suits, and he was booming and laughing away like he was the risen Lord Jesus Himself.

Opinions seemed to be sharply divided about Reverend Roberts' vanishing trick.

One man was jabbing his finger at him.

'God is angry with the wicket!' he was saying. 'Angry with the wicket.'

'Unless a man be born again he cannot enter the kingdom of God,' added another man.

'I agree,' said the Reverend Roberts.

'Acts 18!' he was saying loudly at the Reverend Roberts. 'The Christians renounced magic and the demonic arts.'

'It's not magic,' boomed the reverend. 'I—'

'Beware the serpentine foe of compromise with the world,' interrupted the man.

'Abstain from every form of evil,' said the other.

'I shall,' said the Reverend Roberts, who was taking it all in good part.

'I Thessalonians,' said the man.

'Chapter 5,' said the other.

'Yes,' said the Reverend Roberts. 'Verse 22.'

The two men looked unimpressed.

'How did Jacob deceive Isaac?' one of the men continued.

'"He dressed in Esau's clothes,"' said the other.

'"Cloths",' corrected the Reverend Roberts.

'"Cloths",' continued the man, '"and wore kid skins and brought him savoury meat from two kid goats in order to deceive Isaac."'

'Indeed,' agreed the Reverend Roberts. 'But I was not intending to deceive. It was a demonstration, merely of—'

But the two men had tired of the reverend's justifications and shook their heads and moved away, only to be replaced by other men and women wishing to congratulate and debate with him.

Israel stood quietly eating biscuits – good quality biscuits, actually, maybe bought specially for Easter – and eventually the crowds dispersed and the reverend spied Israel.

'Israel!' he called.

'Yes,' said Israel, going over, not quite sure how you were supposed to greet a minister after a sermon. 'Well done! That was very . . . entertaining.'

'Ho, ho, ho!' boomed the reverend.

'So, how the hell did you do it?'

'My disappearance?' said the reverend. 'I couldn't possibly tell you. Or I could tell, but then I would have to kill you! Ho, ho, ho! No, seriously though. I'll give you a clue: it can only work here in a Baptist church.'

Israel took another bite of his chocolate biscuit – his fifth – and looked blank. 'Why?'

'Because . . .' said the Reverend Roberts. 'Come on! Baptists? Why are they called Baptists?'

'I don't know,' said Israel.

'Baptism?' said the Reverend Roberts.

'What, the little . . . ?' Israel had in mind the kind of stone font at the back of a church.

'No. Not a font!' The reverend laughed. 'No! The Baptists have the full immersion.'

'Do they?' Israel had never come across that before. He didn't mix much with Baptists back home in north London; certainly no Baptist had ever declared themselves to him.

'Yes!' said the reverend. 'In a pool.'

'What, a swimming pool?'

'Yes, well, more like a large bath actually. At the front of the church.'

'Really?'

'Yes. Under the stage. You have to be careful not to slip, you know. And with the microphone, it's very dangerous.'

'Dangerous?'

'Water and electricity. People have died.'

'Bloody hell. Really?'

'Yes. In church.'

'That's ironic, isn't it?'

'God moves in mysterious ways,' agreed the reverend.

138

'So there's a mini swimming pool at the front of the church?'

'Yes: no water in it today though. Didn't bring my trunks! Ho, ho, ho!'

'I see,' said Israel, finishing his biscuit. 'So it was all a set-up?'

'Of course!' The reverend laughed. 'What, did you think it was magic?'

'No! Of course not,' said Israel. He had wondered though; he'd read that Keith Thomas book, *Religion and the Decline of Magic*, when he was at college – good book. Couldn't remember anything about it.

'Do you always do novelty vanishing tricks in your services?'

'Not at all! Sometimes I do juggling!' The reverend laughed and laughed. 'No, no, but seriously. It's good to have some visual aids. It's a trick of the trade.'

'Isn't it a bit odd, though, having magic in a service?'

'Not at all! All things counter, original, spare and strange.'

'Sorry. What's that?'

'Gerard Manley Hopkins? I thought you'd studied English literature?'

'Yes, I did, but I did, erm . . . you know, a lot of twentieth-century American stuff.'

'Ah! Chandler? Spillane? Dashiell Hammett?'

'No, it was more Donald Barthelme.'

'Oh. Well. But what was Jesus, after all?'

'Sorry, is that another quote?'

'No! It's a question! What was Jesus?'

'The Son of God?' said Israel.

'No!' The reverend Roberts laughed. 'He was a wonder-working rabbi, wasn't he?'

'Was he?'

'At the very least,' said the reverend. 'At the *very* least.'

'Right.'

The Reverend Roberts was clearly getting onto a hobby horse here. He had a glint in his eye.

'Also, Israel, in your Hebrew Bible, you know, there's lots of – what shall we say? – jiggery-pokery. Burning bushes, talking donkeys. God wasn't shy of making His point, was He? Even He needs His gimmicks. *Abracadabra,* it's from the Hebrew.'

'Is it?'

'Oh, yes. It's very popular among the clergy these days, magic.'

'Really?'

'Unicycling as well, very popular. There's a bishop over in England who specialises in turning water into—'

'Wine?' said Israel. 'That's very good.'

'No, no, no!' said the Reverend Roberts. 'Even better than that! He turns wine into a sparkling non-alcoholic celebration beverage!'

'Sorry?'

'Shloer,' said the reverend. 'Isn't that *fantastic*! Unlike this coffee,' he added, leaning down towards Israel, 'which tastes like gnat's piss.'

'Yes,' spluttered Israel.

'But my friend,' said the reverend, putting his arm round Israel's shoulder, 'enough about me, how are you?'

Living in Tumdrum Israel had become accustomed to no one asking or being particularly interested in how he was; in fact, he'd almost lost interest himself, and found it increasingly difficult to gauge, though given the events of the past twenty-four hours he had no difficulty in finding the right word to describe how he was feeling at the moment.

'Terrible,' he said.

The reverend was strolling with him over to the door.

'More overdue books?'

'No, God, bloody hell, no – oops, sorry.'

'No offence taken.'

'No, I mean, it's much worse. I have a, er, a missing persons problem of my own to solve at the moment,' said Israel.

'Oh, yes?'

'You know about Mr Dixon?'

'Should I know?' said the reverend.

'He's disappeared.'

'What, Mr Dixon from Dixon and Pickering's?'

'Yes.'

'Oh.'

'And there's been a big robbery there.'

'Really, when was this?'

'Yesterday,' said Israel. 'Yesterday morning.' It seemed like a lifetime ago.

'Paramilitaries?'

'I don't know,' said Israel. 'I'm trying to find out what's happened.'

'Ah! Playing detective again?'

'Not exactly. The police think I may have had something to do with it.'

They were descending the steps at the front of the church.

'You!' The Reverend Roberts laughed.

'Yes, me,' said Israel.

'Ho, ho, ho!' laughed the reverend.

'What?'

'That's very funny.'

'Why?'

'Well, you're a librarian, Israel!'

'Yes,' agreed Israel. 'But they took me in and arrested me. I'm out on bail.'

'Goodness me! Bound with fetters of brass and taken to Gaza!' said the Reverend Roberts.

'Uh-huh.'

'Oh dear, dear, dear. This is grave news indeed.'

'Yes.'

'I know him quite well, actually,' said the reverend.

'Mr Dixon? Really? Do you?'

'Yes. Methodist. Very good-living people, the Methodists. Wouldn't give them houseroom. Ho, ho, ho!'

'How do you know him?'

'Through the North Antrim Society of Magic.'

'The what?'

'He's a brilliant magician. Takes it very seriously.'

'Really?'

'Oh yes. You should probably speak to Walter Wilson. The Wonderful Wilsoni. He and Mr Dixon are old magic friends – go back a long way. You should definitely speak to him. He might have an idea, you know, where to start on your—'

'Inquiry.'

'Precisely. See, you've picked up the lingo – you'll be fine!'

They were standing outside the church. Israel was looking at the empty space where he'd left Brownie's bike.

'My bike!'

'What?' said the reverend.

'I left my bike here.'

'It's not here now.'

'No,' said Israel. 'God! Who'd steal a bloody bike from outside a church. Jesus!'

'I doubt it,' said the reverend.

'Sorry, it's just . . .'

'It's fine.'

'I've got to . . . I've only got a week to prove my innocence,' said Israel.

'I'm sure it won't take that long,' said the reverend.

'But if I can't get around anywhere.'

'Well, I would offer to give you a lift, but' – the

reverend checked his watch – 'I'm afraid I have to meet some of the elders of the church, who are very keen to talk to me, as you may imagine, after my sermon.'

'Yes, of course,' said Israel, desperately trying to think what he needed to do next, and how to get there, and who was going to help him. 'What's the time?'

'It's half past twelve.'

Israel groaned.

'Is there a problem?'

'No. No problem. Just . . . Would you mind if I borrowed your phone? I need to ring someone.'

CHAPTER 9

'The old team, then,' said Ted, when he arrived, triumphant, in his cab to pick up Israel.

'Yes.' Israel was trying to remember Mr Wilson's address.

'Half twelve, didn't I say?'

'Yes, Ted.'

'There you are then. I'll not be hanging around today, mind. I've choir this afternoon,' said Ted.

'You sing in a choir?'

'No, I play trombone in the choir: what do you think I do in a choir?'

'I—'

'In the name of God, man, are you daft in the head?'

'No. Erm. Thanks. Yes. It's just . . .'

'What?'

'You don't strike me as the kind of person who would sing in a choir,' said Israel.

Ted's shaven head bristled at this: veins stood out on his bull-like neck. 'Aye, right,' he said. 'And you don't strike me as the kind of person who'd be arrested on suspicion of robbery and kidnap and unable to dig hisself out of the flippin' hole he's gotten into, but.'

'OK, fair point, yes. Sorry.'

'I should think so.'

'So what is it, a church choir?' said Israel.

'Not at all,' said Ted. 'We're a male voice choir.'

'I thought they were Welsh?'

'Aye, in Wales they are. That's just what you'd know.'

'Well, they are mostly Welsh though, aren't they?'

'Aye, and to a worm in horseradish the world is horseradish.'

'What?'

'It's a saying.'

'Meaning?'

'It's a small world to him that's never travelled.'

'Right.'

'If you'd ever been anywhere you'd know.'

'I've been to lots of places,' Israel protested. He'd been to France. Once. And Israel. And that was it, actually.

'You get choirs everywhere, you witless wonder,' said Ted. 'And we're over a hundred years old here – one of the oldest in Ireland, north or south. Started out with the fishermen, like, once it was into winter, and they'd laid up their nets, and most of them didn't take a drink, but, so they formed the choir. And that's us.'

'Very good,' said Israel doubtfully.

'We're world-famous, you know.'

'Uh-huh.' Israel was looking out of the window

at the desolate housing estates they were passing through: what did a paramilitary mural do to your house price exactly?

'We're away over to Slovenia in the summer for a competition,' said Ted. 'And last year it was South Africa.'

'Really? You're going to Slovenia?'

'Aye.'

'And you went to South Africa?'

'Aye.'

'You're not winding me up?'

'We came second in South Africa. Greece we were in a couple of years ago. They've some lovely singing in Greece.'

'That's amazing. From here, the Tumdrum choir?'

'Aye. That's right. Stick up your snoot at us.'

'My snoot?'

'Aye. Your nose.'

'I'm not sticking up my nose at you.'

'Aye. Well.'

'I'm very interested in your choir, Ted.'

'You are, are ye? Well, you're very welcome to come along.'

'Erm . . .'

'You're not a bass, by any chance? We're short of a bass.'

'No, I don't think so. I've got my hands, er . . .'

'Aye, well, you don't look like a bass.'

'Thanks.'

'You look more like a castrato.'

'Thanks.'

'I'm telling you, boy. You still need a haircut, tame that fuzz. Any longer you'll be lookin' like a woman.'

Israel had rather hoped he was looking more like Bob Dylan.

Ted dropped him off at Mr and Mrs Wilson's house, up at Ballyrankin, which was one of the constellation of stained 1970s concrete estates that fringed Tumdrum like claggy on a sheep's arse; since living here Israel had actually seen the claggy on a sheep's arse, so he felt he could speak authoritatively on the subject. Each house up at Ballyrankin looked exactly the same: it was as though you were looking at a street wallpapered with houses. The Wilsons' house sat slap in the middle of a long repeat-pattern.

Israel rang the doorbell.

An old lady opened the door. She was wearing a cardigan with a Scotty-dog brooch, and a pinny. As far as he could remember Israel had never seen anyone wearing an actual pinny before, except in television dramas. Like many of the women Israel had come across in Tumdrum she also wore a machine-knit sparkly cardigan, and also like many of the women Israel had come across in Tumdrum she seemed both hugely distracted and desperate to talk.

'Erm. Mrs Wilson?'

'Yes.'

'I'm looking for, erm, your husband? The . . . erm, the Wonderful Wilsoni?'

148

'Right. Is it a party?'

'No.'

'You're not after booking a party?'

'No, I'm afraid not.'

'He's not been well, you see.'

'I'm sorry to hear that.'

'Six months we had to wait for that last appointment.'

'Erm . . .'

'We'd have gone private if we could have afforded it, but we'd sold our insurance already, when we had the problems with his pension.'

'I see.'

'And I've not paid my full stamp, you see, so I've had to take a wee job in the chemist's.'

'Uh-huh.'

'Only three afternoons a week, mind, but it makes a difference.'

'Yes,' agreed Israel.

'So. Sorry, you are?'

'I'm Israel Armstrong, the librarian.'

'Ach, aye, of course. Is it the books? I thought I'd took them back.'

'No, no, it's—'

'That Alice Sebold – I really enjoyed that. And the Dave Eggers.'

'Really?'

'Aye. Not a patch on Marilynne Robinson, like, but they're young, aren't they?'

'Yes.'

'Time to develop.'

'Erm . . .'

'Look at Philip Roth.'

'Indeed. It's not the books I've come about though, Mrs Wilson.'

'Is it the DVDs?'

'No, no,' said Israel.

'I told him to take that back. He must have seen that *The Wicker Man* a hundred times. Is it *The Wicker Man*? Or is it one of them ones with Jodie Foster? He's a thing for Jodie Foster.'

'No, no, it's not the DVDs. There's nothing overdue. I just need to talk to him about Mr Dixon.'

'Och, really?'

'Yes, indeed.'

Mrs Wilson stood on the doorstep thinking. 'What would you want to be talking to him about Mr Dixon for?'

'Well, it's a magician thing—'

'Och, aye, right enough. Once you've him started you'll never shut him up, mind. He's out back. He spends hours in there. You know what they're like. Keeps him out of mischief.' Mrs Wilson spoke of her husband, as all the women of Tumdrum seemed to do, as if he were a teenage delinquent.

'Could I . . .'

'Aye, down the passage there, you'll see the shed.'

She pointed Israel down a narrow alley which separated the Wilson household from their perfectly symmetrical neighbours, and he went down the passage and through a gate, and he found himself in a small but immensely tidy garden, filled with small but immensely tidy plants, as if tended by a team of exceptionally tidy and green-fingered gnomes; each blade of grass seemed to have been individually clipped. There were no actual gnomes, as far as Israel could see, but there were lots of small Chinese stone lanterns and concrete statuettes, and he passed a tiny pond with tiny orange fish, and walked down a concrete-flag path, flanked by pansies, to the large shed at the bottom of the garden. There was a bird table outside, and a cold frame filled with budding plants. A light shone inside. Israel tapped on the door.

'Hello?' he called. 'Mr Wilson?'

'Enter!' came the voice from inside.

Israel pushed open the door. Mr Wilson was seated at a workbench at the far end of the shed and had swivelled round to face Israel and was staring at him, frowning. He had a small white goatee beard, and a curiously unlined red-flushed face. He was wearing a collarless shirt and braces, and wore thick tortoiseshell glasses. He looked like a child dressed up as an old man.

'Hello,' said Israel. 'I'm Israel Armstrong, the librarian. Your wife kindly—'

'Aye, right. Is it the DVDs? I told her a dozen times about returning them. She must've seen that *English Patient* . . . goodness knows.'

'No, it's not the DVDs, Mr Wilson.'

'Liam Neeson, she's a thing for him.'

'No, it's nothing to do with Liam Neeson,' said Israel.

'He's a Ballymena man,' said Mr Wilson. 'Her brother knew his uncle.'

'Right, good. Operational headquarters, eh?' said Israel, changing the subject.

'I beg your pardon?'

'This,' said Israel. 'It's . . . erm, a lovely shed.'

'That it is.'

Israel looked around. The shed was crammed from floor to ceiling with small brown lidded cardboard boxes, which were neatly arranged on neat plain pine shelves. Each box was labelled, and the arrangement ran from left to right, starting by the door and running all the way around the room from A to Z. Israel stared at the hundreds of boxes and at the tiny copperplate-lettered labels: 'Anti-Gravity', the boxes began, by the door, then 'Automaton', and on through 'Billiard Balls', 'Bullets', 'Cake (Sponge)', 'Camera (Squirting)', 'Candles (Appearing)', 'Candles (Vanishing)', a dozen boxes of 'Cards', from 'Cards (Double-backed)' to 'Cards (Reversible)', to 'Chicken (Rubber)' and 'Coins (Penetrating)', to 'Cups (& Balls)' brass and plastic, 'Die' and 'Doves', and 'Eggs' and 'Egg Bag', 'Exploding Pens' and 'Fate's Fickle Finger', and 'Flying Carpet' and 'Funnels' and 'Golden Key', 'Guillotine', 'Heads', 'Invisible Thread', to 'Knives (Retractable)', 'Knots' and 'Locks', 'Matchboxes', 'Mirrors', 'Newspaper (Milk)', 'Newspaper (Torn and Restored)', 'Rabbit', 'Rings (Linking)', 'Rope (50')' and 'Rope (20')', 'Silk', 9", 12", 18", 'Sphinx', 'Squeakers', 'Swords (Swallowing)', 'Table Cloth (Black)' and 'Table Cloth (Fringed)', 'Vanishing Bowl', 'Wands' breakable and 5-in-1, 'X-Ray Glasses', 'Yo-yos', and finally, scanning round 180 degrees, something called 'Zig-Zags'. Aladdin's Cave was not the right phrase; it was a mad pharmacopoeia.

'It's very . . . cosy,' said Israel, rubbing his hands together in what he hoped was a friendly 'I've-stepped-into-the-lair-of-a-madman-but-really-that's-fine' kind of a gesture.

'Aye,' agreed Mr Wilson. 'When we had the extension I had the pipes run out here for central heating.'

'I see. It's . . . lovely.'

'But you've not come to discuss my central heating, presumably.'

'No,' said Israel. 'No, I haven't actually. You're right. I came to ask about Mr Dixon.'

'Ah, did you now? The Grand Disappearance.'

'Yes,' said Israel hesitantly. 'You've heard about it then?'

'Is there anyone who hasn't heard about it?'

'It's a small town,' agreed Israel.

'Aye. And you're not from round here?' said Mr Wilson.

'No. No, that's correct.'

'You're from the mainland.'

'Yes,' agreed Israel.

Israel always felt uncomfortable when people in Northern Ireland referred to England as the mainland, not because there was any implied deference, but rather on the contrary; because it was usually spoken with such obvious and utter contempt, the equivalent of a taxi driver addressing you as 'sir' and meaning 'arsehole'.

'I understand you're a magician?' persisted Israel.

'I may certainly count myself among that happy brotherhood,' said Mr Wilson.

'The Wonderful Wilsoni?'

'Indeed.'

Israel could just imagine him in a novelty waistcoat, the tips of his moustache waxed and shining in the stage lights.

'And Mr Dixon,' he said, 'he was a magician also?'

'Aye.'

'And you were friends?'

'You're not the police, sir?'

'No. I'm the librarian.'

'You don't look like a librarian.' Mr Wilson stared hard at Israel, his silvery white goatee shimmering in the fluorescent light, his red cheeks burning.

'Well. I, er . . .' began Israel. Honestly, what did people expect librarians to look like?

'I'd expect a jacket and tie at least,' said Mr Wilson, as if he were reading Israel's mind. 'I suppose everyone's scruffy these days, but.'

'Anyway,' said Israel, 'I just—'

'Do the police know you're here?'

'No. I don't think so.'

'Hmm.'

'I was just wondering how you knew Mr Dixon, whether you knew him well?'

'And why's it your business?'

'Well, you see, the police have . . . erm, they think I might have had something to do with his disappearance—'

'You?'

'Yes.'

'A librarian!' Mr Wilson laughed.

'Yes,' said Israel indignantly.

Librarians are capable of kidnap and robbery, and much worse, probably, thought Israel: Chairman Mao was a librarian, he was about to point out.

'Chairman Mao was a librarian,' said Mr Wilson.

'Yes,' said Israel. 'How did you—'

'Ha!' said Mr Wilson. 'Well, I knew they were desperate, the PSNI, but I didn't realise how desperate.'

'Yes, anyway,' said Israel, 'I'm trying to establish my innocence.'

'I see.'

'Not that it needs establishing,' clarified Israel. 'I mean, I *am* innocent.'

'Aye?'

'Yes.'

'I'll have to take your word for that, won't I?'

'I'm afraid so.'

'So.' Mr Wilson's hands rested across his stomach.

'So I wondered if you'd mind if I asked you a few questions about Mr Dixon.'

'To help an innocent young man clear his name?'

'Well, yes, I suppose that's—'

'Did you ever see the fillim' – he said *fillim* – '*The Shawshank Redemption*?'

'Yes,' said Israel.

'That was a great film.'

'Indeed.'

'So?' Mr Wilson thrummed his thumbs across his belly. 'Go on.'

'Well . . .'

Israel hadn't thought quite this far ahead, but having already been extensively questioned and interrogated himself, he presumed he might be able to find some way of getting the information he needed, although obviously he couldn't ask Mr Wilson to wear a paper suit and provide a DNA sample. That'd be going too far. So instead he tried low-level chat, though there was no low-level chat in any of Brownie's Elmore Leonards, as far as he could recall, but it was worth a go.

'How did you get to know Mr Dixon?'

'Ach, Mr Dixon?' Mr Wilson gazed up at the ceiling of the shed. 'Mr Dixon. The Impossible Mr Dixon.'

'Was he a difficult man?'

'No, that was his stage name. The Impossible Mr Dixon.'

'Right. I see.'

'I've known him a very long time. Right back before you were born.' Mr Wilson stroked his goatee. 'We used to do shows together, you know, works dos and what have you. When I first knew him – this was what? – back in the late sixties I suppose, he was doing card tricks mostly. He was drinking then.'

'Right.'

'We started out with the auld egg and hankie stuff, and then . . .'

'Yes?'

As Mr Wilson was speaking Israel was searching in his pockets for a pencil and some paper.

'You wouldn't have a pen and a piece of paper handy would you, that I could . . .'

'What for?'

'So I can keep a' – Israel continued rootling around in his pockets – 'a contemporaneous record of our . . .'

'Here you are.'

Mr Wilson got up slowly from his seat, went to one of his cardboard boxes, pulled it down, searched around inside and then handed Israel a sheet of paper and a pen.

'Great, thanks. So, where were we?' said Israel, pen poised, once Mr Wilson had sat down.

'You were asking me about how I knew Mr Dixon.'

'Ah, yes. That's right. So . . .'

'He never really had the skills for it, to be honest.'

'For what?'

'The conjuring. Requires a lot of practice. Dexterity, you know. So he moved into illusions. The auld slippery slope. One minute you're doing floating balls and next thing you're sawing a lady in half.'

'Uh-huh. Could you just slow down a little bit, Mr Wilson. My writing, you see, can't . . .'

It wasn't as easy as it looked.

Mr Wilson ignored Israel's request and kept on talking.

'It's all about apparatus, you see, with the illusions. It's not really magic: it's mechanics. Different thing entirely. It's all Las Vegas these days – how much money are you willing to spend. I make all my own tricks right here,' said Mr Wilson, tapping his head.

'Right.'

'As it should be.'

'Good.'

Mr Wilson stared into middle space.

'Mr Dixon?' prompted Israel.

'Aye. I got to know him in the UAM I think it was. Which was a long time ago now of course.'

'Sorry, the UAM?'

'Ulster Association of Magicians. Which had split, you see, from the Irish Friends of Magic. That was – what? – early sixties. We were only kids at the time. I was serving my time in the print-works. He was working in the shop already.'

'Right.'

'And the Irish Friends of Magic had already split from the Irish Magic Circle, I don't know, back in the 1940s.'

'Uh-huh. That's . . . I don't know, that's maybe a little too far back actually . . .'

'It's background,' said Mr Wilson.

'Yes. But . . .'

'You don't want background?'

'Well, it's very interesting, but . . . Anyway, you were in the same magic society?'

'Aye. There was also the Ulster Circle of Conjurors, they were another group that had formed.'

'Right.'

'And the Northern Irish Magic Triangle.'

'Hmm.'

'Though they didn't last long. They got took over by the UCC.'

'The?'

'Ulster Circle of Conjurors.'

'Right. But you two were – what was it?' Israel glanced back at his notes. 'The UAM?'

'Aye. But then there was a split in the UAM.'

'Right. I see. Why was that?'

'It was a disagreement about the direction we were going in as a society. People felt that the whole thing was too much focused down in Belfast.'

'I see.'

'So out of the UAM we formed the North Antrim Society of Magic.'

'Who did?'

'We did.'

'Who, you and Mr Dixon?'

'That's right. And others of course. Some of them left, mind, and formed the North Antrim Magical Society.'

'Right.'

'And the North Ulster Magic Club.'

'There're quite a lot of these magic societies, aren't there' said Israel, staring at his notes. It was quite messy: he thought it was probably his note-taking that had cost him a first in his finals, actually.

'Aye. Always been very popular in these parts.'

'Yes,' said Israel, pushing his spectacles up high on his forehead. 'I was speaking to the Reverend Roberts, actually, from the First Presbyterian Church. It was him who put me on to you. He's a member of the Fellowship of Christian Magicians.'

'Aye, well, we wouldn't really consider them proper magicians.'

'I see.'

'Bunch of clowns.'

'OK. Anyway, just so I've got it clear in my own mind. You and Mr Dixon are in the North Antrim Society of Magic—'

'No. Mr Dixon is not a member of the North Antrim Society of Magic.'

'But, hold on, you just said—'

Mr Wilson fixed Israel with his beady eyes. 'Mr

Dixon *was* in the North Antrim Society of Magic. We're a broad church, not just cardicians.'

'Uh-huh.'

'We've dove magicians.'

'Um.'

'All sorts. Weight-and-motion-resistance specialist, we have. Big girl. Miss Tree. She's from Ballymena.'

'Erm . . .' Israel was having difficulty in seeing the relevance of this to his investigation.

'We even had a paper-tearer, Signor Bob, but he passed on. Dying art, paper tearing. No escape artists at th'moment. They've their own society – the Ulster Escapologists.'

'Good.'

'Down in the Moy. Muldoon, isn't it; the fella?'

'I don't know.'

'Aye. Well. Everything else we have: billiard ball manipulators; regurgitationists. There's a baker over in Derry who specialises in the Bullet Catch. Fella from Armoy who does stuff with ducks.'

'Quite a range then.'

'Ach, aye. We have all sorts. Mentalists.'

'Mentalists?'

'Mind-reading, you know? Couple of fellas up from Belfast.'

'Ah, right. But Mr Dixon?'

'Aye. Well, I'm afraid we had to draw the line somewhere.'

Now, even Israel could tell he was getting close to what he wanted to know.

'What was the problem with Mr Dixon?'

Mr Wilson sighed a long, deep sigh. 'He was getting carried away is the best way I can describe it.'

'Carried away?'

'Aye, you know. He was wanting to put on these big shows all the time, but we weren't ready for it up here. I think because of the store, you see, he thought he was the big shot. Billy Big Shot some of our members used to call him. It was a clash of personalities. He was too flashy for us. He was always wanting to be spectacular.'

'Well, we all want to be spectacular, don't we?' Israel laughed.

'Not round here we don't,' said Mr Wilson, deadpan. 'He was getting more and more into the entertainment side of it. He'd got away from the true spirit of magic. He wanted to do the Donkey Disappears and all sorts.'

'The what?'

'The Donkey Disappears. It's a trick, but.'

'With an actual donkey?'

'Aye,' said Mr Wilson. 'Or whatever. Elephant. Horse. Pigs. He'd buy these things from America: £5,000 he spent, apparently, on some big box, the eejit. He was addicted to conjuring appliances.'

'Right.' Israel noted this down.

'He was a crowd-pleaser.'

'But isn't all magic like that?'

'Not at all! Contraptions? Anyone can do anything with a few contraptions. The true spirit

162

of magic is a wee boy making his own magic. You can't buy magic. It's not about how much money you've got. It's about skills, sleight of hand.'

'I see,' said Israel sceptically.

'Look,' said Mr Wilson.

He got up again slowly from his seat and turned off the light in the shed, switched on a small anglepoise lamp, and drew red and white checkerboard curtains across the tiny window.

Israel was watching him nervously.

'Watch the door,' commanded Mr Wilson.

Israel was starting to feel uncomfortable now, but he dutifully looked at the door – was someone going to come in? – while Mr Wilson stretched his hands and cracked his knuckles, arranged the lamp behind him and carefully closed one hand over another.

A shadow appeared on the door: a swan smoothing its plumage. It was absolutely extraordinary; it was just Mr Wilson moving his hands. He moved his hands again, and there was a shadow of a bird taking flight, and then a duck skidding to a halt, and then a house, a church, a man conducting, an old oak tree, and a dog's head, its snout snapping at some food and then swallowing it.

The show was over in seconds, but it seemed to have lasted for hours.

'Now that,' said Mr Wilson, wriggling his fingers, 'if you'll forgive the cliché, is magic.'

'That's brilliant!' said Israel, genuinely impressed. 'How do you . . . ?'

'It's all in the curve of the thumb,' said Mr Wilson.

Israel tried it. He managed to make a butterfly.

'That's a start, I suppose,' said Mr Wilson.

'Anyway,' said Israel, remembering why he was there. 'Mr Dixon? What happened? He left your organisation?'

'No. He was expelled.'

'Really?'

'Yes. We broke his wand.'

'I'm sorry?'

'When someone breaks fellowship with you as a magician, we break their wand.'

'Really? That's a bit—'

'It's symbolic,' said Mr Wilson.

'How long ago was that exactly?'

'When he left? Years ago now.'

'Oh, right. So you wouldn't have any idea of what might have happened to Mr Dixon at the moment, if he had any enemies or anything . . .'

'Enemies!' Mr Wilson laughed. 'No! I can't help you with any of that sort of thing. As you can see, I'm just an old man surrounded by my books and my tricks.'

'Like Prospero,' said Israel.

'Or Caliban,' said Mr Wilson, his beady eyes staring at Israel.

'Yes. Well, thanks anyway. It's been . . . very helpful.'

Israel turned towards the door.

'But I can tell you this,' said Mr Wilson, who

was hunched over his desk again. 'In magic what you see is the effect, which is produced by the method.'

'Uh-huh.'

'That's what people always want to know: "How did you do that?"'

'Yes.'

'But the actual key to magic is the misdirection.'

'Right.'

'Directing the audience's attention somewhere else.'

'I see.'

Mr Wilson was peering up at Israel, his face shining in the light.

'And that's relevant to me because?'

'If Mr Dixon has everyone thinking he's been kidnapped . . .'

'Yes.'

'Well, my guess is he hasn't been kidnapped at all.'

'Really?'

'You'd need to speak to the wife, I'd think.'

'I would?'

'Behind every great man . . .'

There was a knock at the door of the shed. It was Mrs Wilson, in her pinny.

'Come on!' she said, clapping her hands. 'It's your programme on.'

'Ah, good,' said Mr Wilson. 'Our guest here was just leaving.'

When he consulted his notes back at the Devines' later that night Israel found nothing there: Mr Wilson had given him a pen with disappearing ink.

CHAPTER 10

It certainly took some explaining to George, about Brownie's bike having been stolen from outside the church: Israel had explained, and apologised, and explained again, and George had just looked at him, silently, her arms folded, and in attempting to explain Israel was in fact simply digging himself a larger and deeper hole, and when he thought he'd dug down deep enough George's silence had kept him digging some more.

'I'll pay for it,' he said in the end, breaking light somewhere near Melbourne, Australia.

'Correct,' said George, walking away.

It was the Easter Monday morning and he was no closer to solving the mystery of Mr Dixon's disappearance than he had been on Easter Sunday. He'd sat up half the night again reading Brownie's damp crime fiction but that was still getting him nowhere, so he'd decided to take the Wonderful Wilsoni's advice and go and see Mrs Dixon. It was a high-risk strategy, but he didn't have any others.

Ted was taking the day off, and so Israel, having lost the bike, and the van, and all other forms of transport being unavailable to him – buses in and around Tumdrum being about as rare as hen's teeth – decided to walk, which gave him an opportunity to enjoy Tumdrum's scenery and to review his evidence so far. So far, he had established that Mr Dixon had disappeared, and the fields were certainly looking nice this time of year. On the long wet road down by the sea the endless waves were endlessly lashing against the shore.

The Dixons lived in a house off the main coast road to Rathkeltair; you could just see the house from the road, although it was surrounded on all sides with high white rendered concrete walls, and a protective miniature forest was planted all around it, and at the big black iron gates there were CCTV cameras and a buzzer.

Israel rang.

'Yes?' fuzzed a voice after a few moments.

'Librarian,' said Israel.

'Say again?' fuzzed the voice back faintly.

'Librarian.'

It was amazing really where the word librarian would get you. As a cover it was perfect: no one suspected librarians of anything, except chronic timidity, and dandruff, and the collecting and issuing of books. Saying to someone you were a librarian was pretty much the equivalent of saying to them, 'No, really, I'm no one, tell me about yourself.' 'Librarian' was the perfect disguise.

The gates swung open and Israel walked up a long gravel drive. The house appeared from a distance to be an old, old house but in fact when you got up close you could see that it was pretty much brand spanking new – no more than a couple of years old at the most by the pristine scuffless look of it, and yet brilliantly and pointlessly built to appear old, or Olde, some unspecified ultimate age of Oldness. The Dixons' was not so much a home as an illustrated guide to the history of genteel building, a generically Tudor-Georgian-Victorian-Edwardian mansion (incorporating a glass and steel Modernist conservatory with a swimming pool stuck on the side). Parked outside the house was the traditional black Saab convertible with a cream leather interior.

The front door was flanked by columns – either Doric or Ionic; Israel could never remember his columns – and as he approached the door opened, and a woman stood there staring unsteadily at him.

'Mrs Dixon?' said Israel.

'Yes?' said the woman.

She was wearing a bottle-green tailored suit, of a kind that Israel had thought had long gone out of manufacture, and certainly out of fashion, a suit that might properly be described as a 'power suit', of a kind that might have found favour among dictators' wives in former Soviet republics. Her odd, possibly inimitable Northern-Irish-Euro-chic style was further accentuated by a cream silk scarf knotted at her throat, and the addition of some heavy gold jewellery, and by her eyebrows, which were etched high on her forehead; she looked like an old Catherine Deneuve playing a younger Catherine Deneuve in a film set in the 1980s, in Northern Ireland.

'The librarian?' she said.

'Yes,' said Israel. 'Hello! I'm Israel Armstrong.'

He went to shake hands but Mrs Dixon drew close and kissed him on both cheeks, continental-style. This would have been unusual enough in north London; in Northern Ireland it was nothing less than profoundly shocking. Israel felt like he'd been slapped, or tickled. He detected mints and wine.

'Welcome,' said Mrs Dixon, drawing back and looking out past Israel at the driveway. 'Did you say your name was Israel?'

'Yes.'

'That's a very unusual name.' Her voice seemed a little slurred.

'I suppose it is, yes.'

'And you're on foot, Israel?'

'Yes. The van is . . . It's got a problem with its . . . erm . . . It's broken down. Anyway, your husband—'

Mrs Dixon raised a raised eyebrow even higher at the mention of her husband. 'Yes?'

'He had . . . *has*, sorry, *has* a lot of books overdue.' He'd been rehearsing his story on the way over. 'They're on order for another reader. So I wondered if I might . . .'

'Yes?' Mrs Dixon notched up the etched eyebrow again.

'It's because they're on order for another reader, you see. A very . . . old reader.'

'I see.'

'Who has read all the other books in the library.'

Mrs Dixon simply looked at him.

'It would really be very helpful.'

'Well, in that case, Israel, you'd better come in.'

'It's a lovely house you have here, Mrs Dixon,' said Israel, stepping across the threshold.

The Dixons' house reminded him of his mum and dad's, in the way that an actual building might remind you of a painted plyboard doll's house, or Legoland might remind you vaguely of London, Paris, New York and the Taj Mahal. His parents' house was a kind of miniature, amateur, hobby-ists' flat-pack version of the Dixons': they shared a similar taste in furnishings, though where his mum had dark, heavy reproduction period-style furniture bought from a young man wearing a shirt with a name-tag on it in a brightly lit showroom up at Brent Cross, the Dixons had actual dark, heavy period furniture, presumably bought from a dimly lit antiques showroom from a man with second homes in France and Cork and children at English public schools.

'Can I get you a drink of anything?' asked Mrs Dixon, wobbling slightly.

'Erm. No, thanks. It's a little—'

'Tea, coffee?'

'Ah, right! Well. A cup of coffee perhaps, would be . . .'

'Good,' said Mrs Dixon. She smiled at him warmly, if a little lopsidedly. 'Shall we go upstairs first?'

'Sorry?'

'Upstairs, Israel,' said Mrs Dixon, hand on hip. 'My husband's office is upstairs.'

'Ah, right, yes.'

Mrs Dixon led Israel to the bottom of a proverbial sweeping staircase – the kind that two people might comfortably ascend or descend together, side by side, carrying a piano.

'After you,' said Mrs Dixon, turning to face Israel; she had a habit of staring at you when speaking to you, eyes wide, eyebrows taut, lashes erect, giving you her full, mad, undivided attention, and as a librarian Israel had become accustomed to people not meeting his eye – who wants a librarian to acknowledge your gaze, eye-to-eye, when you're checking out *Viagra for Dummies*? – so he found this rather unnerving. It felt like she was looking straight into his soul.

'Thank you,' he said, his throat dry.

Mrs Dixon followed him closely up the stairs.

'What age are you, Israel?'

'What age am I?' he said, half turning.

'Yes. If it's not a rude question.'

'No, it's . . . I'm twenty-nine.'

'Ah,' said Mrs Dixon with a sigh. 'And you're making the most of it, I hope?'

'Of what?'

'Your youth!' Mrs Dixon laughed.

'Erm,' said Israel. 'Yes. I suppose, I, er . . . You know . . . I . . .'

'You mustn't let it pass you by.'

'No. Quite.'

'The flower of youth fades.'

'Yes.'

'And leaves behind it . . .' Mrs Dixon's voice trailed off.

'I'm sure this must be a very difficult time for you,' said Israel.

'This?'

'With your husband having . . .'

'Ah, yes,' said Mrs Dixon. 'Very difficult time.'

'I'm sure he'll turn up . . . safe,' said Israel.

'I'd really rather not talk about it, thank you,' said Mrs Dixon huffily.

'Yes, of course,' said Israel.

Family photographs lined the stairway going up. At the very top of the stairs was a black and white photographic portrait of a man and woman in evening dress, holding what appeared to be miniature banjos.

'That's a lovely photo,' said Israel.

'Yes,' agreed Mrs Dixon. 'They were my parents.'

'Oh, right. They were banjo players?'

'Ukuleleists.'

'Right.'

'The Bells?' said Mrs Dixon hopefully. 'Bill and Antoinetta?'

'Uh-huh.'

'They were very famous locally.'

'I see.'

'My mother was French,' said Mrs Dixon, as though this explained every failing and success in her life.

'Really?' Well, that explained the kissing, at least. That, and a bottle or two of early morning Chardonnay.

'Come!' commanded Mrs Dixon, heels clicking, leading Israel down a long corridor decked on either side with paintings – *actual* paintings, rather than reproductions – towards the rear of the house, where she opened a door.

'Here we are, young man.' She didn't enter the room herself, but gestured for him to enter. 'Please? Now, you know what you're looking for?'

'Yes. I think so,' said Israel.

'Good. The books will be over there, somewhere,' she said, indicating shelves. 'I'll go and get you that coffee.'

'Right. Thanks. Yes. I shouldn't be . . .'

Mrs Dixon had gone, leaving behind her just the smell of perfume and dry white wine.

Israel had absolutely no idea what he was looking for. He was hoping something would make itself apparent – a clue.

In Brownie's crime novels the detectives solved mysteries by using a combination of profound reasoning, forensics, sidekicks, and their extraordinary natural resources of intuition and intelligence, intelligence that manifested itself only, it had to be said, in solving grisly and improbable crimes, because when not solving crimes they seemed to spend all their time drinking, smoking and listening to their favourite music ad nauseam. Did none of them ever get a little bit tired, or hungry, or suffer from mild headaches?

Israel gazed desperately around the room, trying to think detectively. How long did he have? How long did it take to make a cup of coffee?

Opposite, the bookshelves. Israel liked to think he was something of a connoisseur of shelves. These were oak, as far as he could tell; they looked like oak, plain, simply finished, not too many frills. Nice. If he had a spare few thousand they were exactly the sort of shelves he might have had installed back in the chicken coop. On these fine sleek shelves of oak there were books of magic, and more books of magic, and nothing but books of magic – legions, thousands, row upon row. There were dozens of *Principles* and *Secrets* of magic, and encyclopaedias and dictionaries and guides and histories and illustrated histories of magic, and biographies of magicians, and bibliographies of magical books. Mr Dixon's vast collection of magic books was fully representative, like a complete library of the world, except this was a world made up only of sleight of hand and trickery, the world made over and revealed in all its deceptions. There was volume upon volume of something called *Card College* and books by Kreskin and by Randi and by other men with improbable names. Was there ever a magician named Smith? One shelf – about 8 foot long – a full stretch – seemed to contain only books by and about Houdini: *Who Was Houdini?*, *This is Houdini*, *The Life of Harry Houdini*, *The Death of Harry Houdini*, *The Lives and Deaths of Harry Houdini*, and one called simply *Houdini!*, and another *Houdini!!*, and another, finally, *Houdini!!!* Another shelf was filled with books about someone called Dante – not the thirteenth-century Italian poet, but a man with a little forked beard who appeared to have been 'The World's Greatest Master of Mystery' back some time when only black-and-white photos were available. Half a dozen shelves of the library contained videos and DVDs – box-sets upon box-sets of the work of a man called Richard Osterlind, and another, Juan Tamariz, and Banachek, whoever he was, and men called Chad and Jay and Tad, all of them acclaimed as Masters and Lords and Kings of their realms; it was like discovering a parallel universe of other Shakespeares. Other shelves were weighed down with what appeared to be entire runs of magic magazines – all the way down from a big glossy called *Magic*, through *Abracadabra*, and *Genii*, down to queer little things called *The Crimp* and *Dr Faustus's Library*.

Clue, clue, God grant him a clue.

A book caught his eye. He took down a copy of Houdini's *The Right Way To Do Wrong*. He flicked through, looking for some inspirational, magical passage.

Nope. No good.

Table in the centre of the room; globe, atlases, travel books: Eric Newby, Jan Morris, Bill Bryson.

Clue, clue, where are you?

At the far end of the room there was a mirrored built-in wardrobe, the kind of thing you might find in a dance studio, or a suburban semi. Israel quickly slid open a mirrored door. Inside: magician's cloak, tails, top hats, rack of wands, sparkly stiletto shoes, sequinned bodices . . .

Well, that was interesting. And beside the mirrored wardrobe, just behind the door, was a little collection of photographs that caught Israel's eye: photos of a man in tails, Mr Dixon, pulling a rabbit from a hat; Mr Dixon in tails with a lovely assistant; Mr Dixon with another lovely assistant; and another; and all the lovely assistants sporting little else but sequinned body suits, ostrich feather boas, white gloves and sparkly stilettos. In their make-up and headdresses and plunging outfits all the women looked the same. Except for one. He thought he recognised the face. He stood on tiptoe and looked close, at the . . . Was that? No, it couldn't be.

'Nice photos, aren't they?' said Mrs Dixon, who had appeared behind Israel, holding two mugs of coffee. 'Here.' She handed him a mug. The coffee smelt good.

'Thanks,' he said. His heart was pounding.

'So, did you find what you were looking for?'

'Erm. No. I mean yes. Actually, I . . .'

The smell of wine seemed mixed now with something stronger – a wee snifter. Mrs Dixon gazed at the photos. The snifter and the photos seemed to put her in the mood to talk.

'The police say if he's not been kidnapped then we have to face the possibility that he has some mental health problem,' she said, looking at the photos. 'It's just—' She broke off, choking with tears.

Israel didn't carry handkerchiefs.

'Shall I get you a . . . Do you want a . . . ?'

'No, thanks,' said Mrs Dixon, dabbing at her eyes. 'The police, you see, it's been very . . . They've been asking all sorts of questions.'

'I'm sure it's been very difficult.'

'Yes, yes. They'll be here again in a minute, actually.'

'Who? The police?'

'Yes, they're coming back this morning. There's a press conference this afternoon.'

'Really?'

'Yes. Sergeant Friel, he's very sweet, he's an old family friend, but—'

There was the sound of ringing downstairs.

'That'll be him,' said Mrs Dixon. 'Excuse me, Israel, won't you? I'll just be a minute. You relax there.'

Relax? Sergeant Friel was not going to be happy to see him. Israel had to get out.

There was a window at the far end of the room. Sash window. He ran across and threw it open.

Looked out. Short drop down onto sloping roof. Should be fine. Better than being caught tampering with evidence by Sergeant Friel.

He started levering himself onto the window ledge. And then he remembered the photograph. He hurried back across the room, behind the door. Was that? It certainly looked like it. But he couldn't be quite sure. He'd have to . . . He took the picture off the wall, and ran back to the window.

By the time Sergeant Friel walked into Mr Dixon's study, Israel was hobbling as fast as his chubby little legs could carry him back down the Dixons' long gravel drive. He'd twisted his bloody ankle. Again.

'Here we are, Sergeant,' Mrs Dixon was saying. 'The librarian.'

But the room was empty.

'That's funny,' said Mrs Dixon. 'He was here a moment ago. He seems just to have disappeared.'

'Aye,' said Sergeant Friel, going over to the window. 'Not for long, Mrs D. Not for long.'

CHAPTER 11

It was a fair walk to the Myowne mobile home park – actually, no, it was much much more, and much less than a fair walk, it was a long, bedraggling, ankle-aching hike along the main unpavemented coastal road, sprayed by cars along one side, spumed by the sea on the other. And when Israel finally made it Rosie wasn't home, so he went down onto the beach, through the drifting grassy dunes, and past the big black rock with the words 'JESUS IS THE ROCK OF MY SALVATION' daubed on it in red gloss letters four feet high, and to be honest he felt like throwing himself upon the mercy of the Lord, or in the sea.

But there she was, Rosie, his rock and his salvation, in the howling wind, her son Conor and her other little charges running around her, digging with buckets and spades, throwing sand, building castles. Rosie looked after other people's children to make money during the day, and she worked in the First and Last at night, and when she had a spare couple of hours she helped Israel out on the mobile library; she was no slacker and no slouch. But even from a distance she looked

beaten. You could tell she was tired; it was something in the give of the shoulders, in the way she
held her head.

'Hey!' shouted Israel as he drew near to her.
'Rosie!' The wind threw the words back in his
face. 'Rosie!' he called again, coming closer.

She must have heard him.

'Rosie!'

She'd definitely heard him.

'Rosie!'

He was standing right by her now, next to her.

She didn't move. She was looking straight ahead,
out to sea. She was wearing her black leather biker
jacket and a green gypsy skirt, and her old brown
leather boots. Her dark, shoulder-length hair was
tucked behind her ears and her fingernails were
painted a purply red, like bruises at her fingertips.
Israel was standing so close to her he could smell
her perfume – he'd almost forgotten what it smelt
like, perfume. He could hear her breathing. A
terrible shiver ran through him.

'Rosie?' Israel gently put a hand on her shoulder.
'Rosie?'

'Get your hands off me!' She pushed his hand
away.

'What?'

'You heard.'

'Rosie, I need to talk to you.'

'Well, I don't want to talk to you.'

'Why?'

'Because you,' she said, 'need to *fucking* wise up.'

She put her hand over her mouth. 'Now look what you've made me do!'

'What?'

'Cursing in front of the children.'

'Rosie, I'm sorry.'

He didn't even know what he was apologising for.

Israel could hear the waves. The seagulls. The wind in his ears. The children, wrapped up warm in their coats and in wellies, laughing, falling down, rolling around in the sand.

'Sorry,' he repeated.

'Not good enough.'

'Look, I'm sorry, I've not . . . It's been a bit hectic the past couple of days.'

'A bit?' said Rosie, unsmiling.

'Well, more than a bit.'

'Aye, well, I've had a *bit of a hectic* few days myself,' she replied, her voice full of sarcasm. 'I had that bitch from the council on the phone.'

'Who?'

'The wee Chinky.'

'Linda?'

'Her.'

'Rosie, you can't call her the wee Chinky.'

'I can call her what I bloody well like.'

'But that's—'

'You lied to me, Is.'

'About what?'

'About me working on the mobile with you.'

'No, I didn't.'

'You were paying me out of the petty cash!'

'Well . . .'

'You told me it was all sorted with the council, that it was all above board and—'

'Yes, well, I . . .'

'What did you think you were doing?'

'I was just . . .'

'What?'

'I just wanted to . . . help you out, you know.'

'Ach, go away!' said Rosie, pushing Israel, physically repelling him. 'You make me sick!'

For a moment Israel thought about turning around and walking away.

'But, Rosie, I—'

'Don't patronise me.'

'I'm not patronising you.'

'Yes, you are! You're patronising me now, you prick!'

'Prick!' shouted Conor, who was listening to every word. 'Prick!'

'Stop that, Conor!' yelled Rosie to the child. 'Right this minute!'

Conor ran off up the beach.

'Look, if you could just . . .' began Israel. 'If you weren't so . . . emotional maybe I could—'

'Emotional? Emotional?' Rosie turned to face him now. 'What's that supposed to mean?'

'Just—'

'Don't you *dare* start telling me what I should feel!'

'I'm not. I'm just—'

'You don't even know what emotional is.'

'Well, yes, I do, but—'

'What is it then?'

'Sorry?'

'I want you to tell me, Israel Armstrong. I want to know what you think. *You*.' She jabbed a finger at him and was staring at him so hard he couldn't maintain eye contact and had to look away. 'Huh? Go on, then. What is it? What's an emotion?'

Israel had been asked a lot of questions since he'd arrived in Tumdrum – mostly whether it would be possible to overlook a fine, or whether there were any extra copies of the books that were part of the Richard and Judy book club – but what is an emotion? That was a tough one. And his answer to this? Israel Armstrong, BA (Hons), his answer to this most simple and searching of questions?

Total silence.

'Well?' persisted Rosie, still looking him in the eye. 'What do you think it is?'

Israel couldn't answer. He was blinking back tears.

'Why are you talking like this?' he said.

'Talking like what?'

'You're angry.'

'Yes, of course I'm angry! Just because I live where I live and do what I do doesn't mean I don't have any self-respect.'

'No, of course not.'

'So why would you treat me like some . . . plaything?'

'I wasn't treating you like a plaything.'

'Well, that's what it looks like to me.'

'No, no. That's not right at all. I was just . . . It's only Linda who has a problem with you helping on the library.'

'Don't try and blame her!'

'I'm not trying to blame her. I'm trying to explain. She said I couldn't have you helping on the library because of insurance and the health and safety and—'

'You should never have had me on the library in the first place if you hadn't sorted it out properly!'

'No. I maybe . . . wasn't thinking straight.'

'Typical male.'

'No, don't say that.'

'Typical male,' she repeated. 'Thinking with your—'

'No!' said Israel. 'Look I just need to—'

'I'll tell you what you need to do!' said Rosie. 'You need to grow up.'

Oh, God. Israel had heard that one before. Gloria had said that to him before.

Israel had always thought that growing up was simply something that happened to you: you grew taller, more dextrous, you acquired language, learned to feed yourself, developed intellectually, went to school, got a mortgage, had children, got fatter and tired and full of regrets, and that was it, you were grown up, you were an adult. There was more to it than that though, apparently – and it was something that women knew, and men did not.

The children were throwing great handfuls of filthy grey sand at each other.

'I don't know what else to say.'

'Don't say anything then.'

'But, Rosie . . .'

'What?'

'It's just . . . I need to ask you something.'

She laughed – a bitter, bitter laugh. 'Go on then, you ask me something.'

'Look, I don't want to . . . here. Do you want to . . .' Israel nodded his head towards her mobile home, up at the edge of the dunes.

The wind and the drizzle had now intensified and were strong enough even by Tumdrum standards to be considered inhospitable.

'All right,' agreed Rosie. 'Let's go.'

She called the children, and started to gather up the buckets and spades. Israel went to help.

'I'll do it,' she said.

'Are you arguing with my mom?' asked Conor, who watched too much American TV.

'No, we're just talking,' said Israel.

'Are you though?'

'No.'

'Are you?'

'No!'

'Is!' said Rosie.

'Sorry.'

In the mobile home Rosie settled the children

down to playing with some dressing-up clothes and sat on her kitchen stool and lit a cigarette.

'Well?' she said. 'Converse.'

Her hair was wet. Israel was chilled to the bone. She did not offer him a cup of tea; she'd usually offer him a cup of tea.

'Sorry,' said Israel. 'I'm just . . . finding all this a little difficult.'

'That's because it is *difficult*.' Rosie sighed, and it was a sigh so heavy, so full of disappointment, a sigh that seemed as though she had paid for it with her whole life as a woman, that Israel felt ashamed all over again. 'You've let me down,' she continued wearily. 'I thought I could trust you.'

'You can trust me.'

Rosie laughed and blew smoke up towards the ceiling.

'I . . .' Israel was about to speak but Rosie shook her head and waved a hand at him to stop speaking, and Israel could see from the way she lowered her head and the catch in her breath that she was about to cry.

There was the sound of laughter as the children at the other end of the room tried on fairy wings and floppy hats and scarves and plastic glasses and firemen's helmets.

Eventually Rosie stubbed out her cigarette in a saucer brimming with butts, ashes and Cellophane. She was ready to talk.

'So, what is it?'

'I . . .' Israel removed the photograph from

187

under his suit jacket where he'd kept it dry on his long hike from the Dixons' and held it out to her.

'It's a photo,' she said.

'Yes.'

'So?'

'It's a photo of you,' said Israel. 'Isn't it?'

'Yes.'

'I took it from Mr Dixon's house earlier today.'

'What?'

'It's a long story . . .'

To the accompanying sound of the children playing doctors and nurses, and cowboys and Indians, Israel explained to Rosie what had happened to him: the theft at the department store; Mr Dixon's disappearance; his arrest. Rosie listened and when he'd finished she lit another cigarette, looked out of the big window at the strand, shook her head and said, 'Jesus! I thought I'd had a bad week!'

And Israel laughed. And she laughed, and when she laughed she threw her head back and her shoulders dropped, and Israel thought it was the most wonderful thing that had ever happened to him. Suddenly they were friends again.

'Tea?' she said.

'I thought you'd never ask.'

Rosie filled the kettle. Israel could breathe easy again.

'So why didn't you tell me?' he asked.

'Tell you what?'

'That you were one of Mr Dixon's assistants.'

'Why would I tell you?'

'I don't know.'

'Well then.'

'Why did you do it?'

'Why do you think? It was easy money. All you had to do was dress up and look glamorous.'

'Did you not mind?'

'Why would I mind?'

'Dressing up in, you know . . .'

'Why? Your girlfriend not dress up for you?'

'Erm . . .' Israel blushed. 'So what's he like?'

'Mr Dixon? He's OK. Quiet sort of fella. Polite, you know. This was a couple of years ago though I was helping him out.'

She put some teabags into mugs.

'I know her better actually.'

'Mrs Dixon?'

'Aye. She runs these little investment clubs.'

'What sort of investment clubs?'

'It's a women-only thing, you know.'

'Right.'

'You pay her money, and she invests it for you, and you get a return from people who—'

'Oh, God, no,' said Israel.

'What?'

'That's a money-tree scheme.'

'A what?'

'My dad used to – he was an accountant – there were always people who would try and set up these schemes, where you pay some money, and then people pay money to you, and so you quadruple or whatever your original investment.'

'That's right. That's what it is.'

'But the schemes always collapse. Because eventually people run out of people to give them the money. It's like pyramid selling.'

'No, Is, it's not. No, it's a proper—'

'You've not paid money into it, have you?'

'Er . . . Well . . .'

'Oh, no.'

'It's all above board. There's loads of people, church people and everything, who—'

'Have you had your payout yet?'

'No, not yet. It's the end of the month I should get it.'

'How much?'

'Well, I invested . . . well, pretty much all my life savings.'

'Oh, God, Rosie. How much?'

'Nearly £2,000.'

'Oh, shit.'

'But I'm getting at least £5,000 back. I'm going to get a wee deposit for a flat.'

'Oh, no, Rosie. It's a scam.'

Rosie tutted. 'Is! Don't be ridiculous! Mrs Dixon running a scam? She's a Methodist.'

Rosie's phone rang. She picked it up. It was Jimmy, up at the reception. The police had arrived at the Myowne mobile home park and were on their way to Rosie's.

'Is!' said Rosie.

'Police?' he said.

'What? You mean you were expecting them?'

'Look, Rosie, I've got to get away.'

'You could have mentioned!'

'Yes, but—'

'But what about your tea? Where are you going to go?'

'I'm going to find Mr Dixon.'

When Sergeant Friel knocked at Rosie's door moments later he was met by a group of little boys and girls wearing plastic police helmets, and Rosie offering him a cup of tea. Israel was already halfway down the beach.

CHAPTER 12

The police press conference had been scheduled to take place in Tumdrum primary school, but the headmaster, Tony Thompson, had refused permission; it was not appropriate, he felt, for the school to be used for such purposes. He didn't mind the occasional community group using the premises for charity events, or amateur dramatics, or martial arts, or the school's use as a polling station at local and general elections, but he drew the line at Tumble-Tots and dog-training, which were too messy and attracted undesirable elements, and a full-scale police investigation into a robbery, kidnap and a potential murder was clearly absolutely out of the question, not something he wanted to expose the children to, though admittedly most of them watched much worse on television every afternoon and evening, when they weren't playing Grand Theft Auto. The PSNI had then put in a request to set up in the First Presbyterian church, but the Reverend Roberts had refused permission also.

As Sergeant Friel then explained to Linda Wei, Deputy Head of Entertainment, Leisure and

Community Services at Tumdrum and District Council, what the police were looking for was a space – not a particularly big space – where they could hold press briefings and set up their operational headquarters. The station in Tumdrum had been shut down after the Good Friday Agreement, the nearest station was now in Rathkeltair, and what they were really looking for was somewhere centrally located in Tumdrum, a neutral territory, where people would be happy to come and speak in confidence. It needn't be a room. It could even be a large vehicle . . .

So, with Linda's blessing, the mobile library had been requisitioned and was now parked in Tumdrum's main square.

The police had erected an awning on the side of the vehicle, so going in to the press conference felt like entering a Bedouin tent, although instead of rugs and cushions and Colonel Gaddafi offering platters of dates and pitta bread and the olive branch of peace, there was a rusty urn with hot water for tea and coffee, paper plates of biscuits, and rows of orange plastic stackable chairs.

A long trestle table had been set at the back of the tent, up by the side of the van, and underneath the words 'Mobile Library' a big poster had been stuck up saying 'Crimestoppers'.

The tent was packed to its considerable capacity, crawling with reporters and cameramen. Veronica Byrd was sitting at the back towards the entrance, and the damp man next to her wore an old tweed cap, thick black glasses, and sported sideburns and a 1970s-style moustache; he was not national press, obviously, and so hardly someone that Veronica needed to talk to, so she stuck to punching things into her BlackBerry and texting on her mobile phone. The man leant across.

'Erm . . .'

'Israel?' said Veronica.

'Sshh,' said Israel. 'You're not supposed to be able to recognise me!'

'Why are you wearing those funny clothes and the stick-on moustache?'

He'd grabbed what he could from the children's dressing-up box on the way out of Rosie's caravan.

The last time Israel and Veronica had met had been some months ago, when Veronica's boyfriend was about to come home, and they had shared a brief, unsuccessful romantic entanglement.

'It's a kind of a joke,' said Israel. 'It's a . . . *Day of the Jackal* theme . . . party thing . . . I'll explain to you later. You wouldn't have a pencil or something I could borrow?'

Veronica looked at him.

'Pen, even?' said Israel. 'Just to make notes.'

'I don't carry spares,' said Veronica.

'Anything?' said Israel.

She dug into her handbag and gave him an eyebrow pencil. It was quite thick.

'Any paper?'

Veronica ostentatiously ripped a sheet of paper from her spiral-bound reporter's notebook.

'Now that's it. Don't ask me for anything else. I'm working here!'

So, the ingeniously disguised Israel was ready for his first police press conference, with eyebrow pencil and a single sheet of paper.

Several policemen emerged from inside the mobile library into the tent – Israel slunk down low in his seat at this point – and sat down at the table. A police officer introduced himself as a detective sergeant and began the briefing.

'Thank you for coming this afternoon, ladies and gentlemen. As you are aware there's a lot of police activity in and around Tumdrum currently in relation to incidents at the weekend at Dixon and Pickering's department store. This is a fast-moving inquiry, and we are grateful both to the press and to the public for their cooperation with us so far in our investigation. We are making an appeal for new information this afternoon, and we're grateful to you for your assistance in this matter. As you know, most major crimes are solved with the help of ordinary members of the public' – unlike in Brownie's detective novels, thought Israel. 'So we want to get as much information out there to the public as we can.'

'Yeah, sure,' murmured a reporter.

'Can I say first of all that this is a major operational challenge for the officers of the PSNI locally, and Tumdrum and District police are doing a magnificent job.'

'Who's helping?' shouted out a reporter.

The detective sergeant ignored the interruption and continued. 'We understand that rumours are sweeping the local area, but the facts of last Easter Saturday morning, so far as we have been able to establish them, are these: Mr Dixon, dressed, we believe, as normal in a dark grey suit and white shirt and tie, left his home at approximately six fifteen. He then got into his silver Mercedes SL600, registration DIX 01, and drove to Dixon and Pickering's department store, where he entered the building using his swipe card. What we are trying to find out is what happened next.'

'That's what we're all trying to find out,' muttered another reporter.

'Mr Dixon has not used his mobile phone, credit cards or cash-machine cards since Saturday, and his passport and his clothes are still at home. I can also confirm that a large sum of money, in cash, is missing from the department store.'

The detective sergeant then paused and glanced behind him. A police officer appeared at the entrance of the mobile library and nodded. You could feel the crowd bristling with excitement: this was the bit everyone seemed to have been waiting for.

'Now at this stage in the inquiry, ladies and gentlemen, Mr Dixon's family wish to make a statement. There *will not* be questions at this stage for the Dixon family. Thank you.'

Mrs Dixon and the Dixons' three daughters emerged from the steps of the mobile library and took up seats with the policemen behind the table.

'Cordelia, Regan and Goneril,' Israel whispered to Veronica.

'Sshh,' said Veronica.

All the Dixon daughters, who appeared to be in their early twenties, looked exactly like their mother: so much so that they might have been a set of Catherine Deneuve Russian dolls. They were all blonde, and they all looked as though they had recently been weeping.

Mrs Dixon was resplendent in a black trouser suit with a dash of colour in the vermilion scarf around her neck. She blew her nose and tearfully read out a statement, which consisted of an appeal for her husband's safe return. The Dixons were then escorted back into the mobile library, and the detective sergeant invited questions.

Veronica had her hand up already.

'Veronica Byrd, the *Impartial Recorder*. Do you suspect paramilitary involvement in the disappearance of Mr Dixon?'

'We're not ruling anything out at this stage of the inquiry.'

'And you're not ruling anything in?'

'That's right. We are working with our partners in Serious Crime, and Interpol, and the National Missing Persons Helpline.'

'Is it kidnap?'

'As I said, we have been very busy analysing

CCTV tapes and taking numerous statements and conducting house-to-house inquiries and at this stage we are keeping an open mind.'

'So you've got no idea?'

'At this stage it's too early to provide a definitive—'

'So you're not yet treating this as kidnap?'

'We can't say at this time.'

'Is this another example of Northern Ireland's mafia-style crime spree?' called out another reporter.

'I can't comment on that at this time.'

'And what about reports that Mr Dixon may have committed suicide?'

'We shall be providing regular updates on the inquiry as it develops, and we would be grateful if you would allow us to conduct our investigations with care and sensitivity during what is obviously an extremely difficult time for the Dixon family.'

The questions dragged on. Israel tried and failed to squeeze some profound sort of insights from the detective's vague assurances. After the press conference there was a gathering of journalists outside, gaggles of men in puffa jackets and cameramen packing up their gear. Veronica was talking to a well-fed-looking man in a trench coat.

A helicopter went overhead. Israel ducked.

'*Apocalypse Now*,' he said, sidling up to Veronica.

'Sorry?' said Veronica, who'd been doing a good job of ignoring him.

'I said, *Apocalypse Now*, you know, the, erm . . .'

'Look, I'll get back to you on that,' said the other reporter, pointing a finger at Veronica as though he were cocking a gun.

'Blast!' said Veronica.

'What?' said Israel.

'I've lost him now! He's from London! *The Times*? What do you want?' said Veronica.

'You're looking well,' said Israel.

'You're looking . . . weird.'

'Thanks. Veronica. Look. I wonder, could I . . .'

'Yes? What?' She had her mobile phone to her ear.

'Ask you a few questions?' said Israel.

'It's me who asks the questions,' said Veronica, waiting for someone to pick up on the other end.

'Yes,' said Israel. 'Sure. But—'

'What is it?'

'Who do you think did it, then?' said Israel.

'Did it? I don't know. I think they've had several people in for questioning already.'

'Yes,' said Israel. 'I was one of them.'

'You!' Veronica laughed.

'Yes, me,' said Israel.

'You are joking, are you?'

'No, I'm not.'

'But you're just a—'

'Librarian,' said Israel wearily. 'Yes, that's right.'

'So why did they take you in for questioning?'

'I—'

'Hello?' Someone had answered Veronica's call.

'Was there,' said Israel.

'What?' said Veronica, holding the phone away from her ear.

'At Dixon and Pickering's. On Saturday morning. When it all happened I was there.'

'You are joking?'

'No.'

'Shit,' said Veronica, then, speaking into the phone, 'Listen, sorry, I'll have to call you back.'

She looked at Israel intently: it was rather unnerving, but, he had to admit, flattering at the same time.

'Can you tell me all about it?'

'If you help me out.'

'You'll show me yours, if I show you mine?'

'Something like that.'

'Well?' said Veronica, hand on hip. 'You're going to show me yours?'

'No, you first.'

'Ach! Israel! You're just like all the others.'

Israel blushed. 'So, what do you know about Mr Dixon?' he asked.

'What do you want to know?'

'I don't know. Anything,' said Israel.

'I know he'd wear the same suits every day. Same shirts. Same shoes.'

'What, he'd never wash them?'

'No, he had several pairs of each, all exactly the same. That's what people say, anyway.'

'Why would someone wear the same clothes every day?'

'I don't know. It's a disguise I suppose, isn't it? Which you would know more about than me, frankly.'

'Yes. Thanks.' Israel fingered his stick-on moustache. 'And what about money trees? Do you know anything about money trees?'

'Money that grows on trees? Hello? Calling Israel?'

'No, I mean those investment schemes, where people—'

'Oh, you mean like pyramid selling?'

'Exactly.'

'Oh yeah, we get those occasionally.'

'Recently, round here?'

'I don't know. They tend not to come to light until the whole thing's collapsed, and then people are too embarrassed to come forward and admit that they've been involved. There was one in a church, I think, a few years back. There's probably been some stuff in the paper. I don't think I've ever done a story on it myself. I could check. Why do you want to know?'

'It's just . . . something I'm working on.'

'Uh-huh.'

'Would you be able to get some information on them?'

'I could. But what's in it for me?'

'You get my full story, when it's all over and done with.'

'Ah, Armstrong,' said Veronica, 'you are a good boy. You know the way to a girl's heart.'

Alas, thought Israel, he did not.

CHAPTER 13

The back room at the the First and Last –
which was run by the famously rude and
teetotal Elder Agnew Jr, and which was
either Tumdrum's first or last pub, depending on
which way you were coming into town – didn't
look as though it had been touched since about
1950, and if it had, the touch had been light, the
wrist limp. Elder, as a born-again evangelical
Christian, did not regard cleanliness as in any way
related to godliness – he believed in justification
by faith and not sanctification by works – and he
was just too mean to pay a cleaner. In the back
room of the First and Last dust had long since
turned to crust, and there was a slight stickiness
to every surface. The front bar of the First and
Last at least made a pretence of a few home
comforts: velveteen banquettes, the occasional
wipe of a surface, pictures, Scripture-text mirrors,
the fire. But in the back room there just was a
single grimy 'Guinness Is Good For You' print on
the wall, an old jukebox, a boarded-up fireplace,
and that was it. Bare boards, tables and chairs
that did not match, primitive wooden benches,

windows with grilles over them, smoke so thick and so dense it felt you were eating it, and you were so close to the vat of Elder's illicit mini-distillery out back that you only had to stay in the room for about half an hour and even if you were drinking sparkling mineral water your eyes would soon start to roll, your spirits soar, your speech slur, and eventually you'd pass out.

Ted was introducing Israel to a few people; he'd been lying low during the afternoon at the offices of the *Impartial Recorder* with Veronica, working his way through the microfiche; he hadn't discovered as much as he'd hoped.

'Big Red, Israel Armstrong.'

'Hello.' Israel and Big Red shook hands.

Big Red had a ginger moustache.

'This is One Brow.'

'Hello.' Israel and One Brow shook hands.

One Brow had one brow.

'Barney.'

Barney sported both comb-over and moustache.

'Hi, Barney.'

Israel went to shake Barney's hand.

'All right, forget the shaking of hands,' said Ted, 'or we'll be here all flippin' night.'

'Sorry, Ted,' said Israel.

'Jim Savage,' continued Ted.

Israel simply nodded. Savage by name, savage by . . .

'This is Thompson – we call him Tonky,' said Ted.

'Hello, Tonky.' Tonky looked withered from drink.

'And Tonky's son, Honky.'

'Honky Thompson?'

'Aye.'

'Hello, Honky.' Honky hadn't yet withered as much as his dad, but he was getting there; he'd shrivelled.

'Wesley you might know. He runs Virtual Victuals.'

'What?'

'Virtual Victuals, the Internet butcher?'

'Irish bacon. Irish hams, black puddings, white puddings,' said Wesley.

'Lovely,' said Israel.

'And Billy,' concluded Ted, nodding towards a man seated at a table with a group of other men, 'and Sammy. And Billy. Sammy. Billy.'

'Billy, Sammy, Billy, Sammy, Billy?'

'Aye.'

'You'll be set a test on the names later,' said a Billy.

'Which I'll fail!' joked Israel.

'Aye,' agreed Ted. 'Drinks then?'

'I'm a bit . . .' Israel patted his pockets.

'Aye. Put your money away.'

Israel accompanied Ted to the bar, which was a plank of wood across the back of the front bar.

Ted ordered.

'Ted.' Israel spoke quietly. 'Who the hell are all these people?'

'These boys? Some of them are from the choir I was telling you about, some of them from the lodge.'

'The Orange lodge?'

'Give over. Masonic lodge.'

'Right. And they're here because?'

'We're putting our minds together to try and help you out. Brainstorming, you know.'

'Brainstorming? No, Ted, look, that's very kind of you and everything, but I'm not sure that's going to help. I don't think we're going to solve this by committee.'

'Aye, right. So how far have you got on your own then, Detective Inspector Rebus?'

'Erm. Well, I think . . .' Israel lowered his voice and looked around to check that no one could overhear him. 'I think there's a possibility Mrs Dixon might be involved in some kind of financial mismanagement.'

'What, she's topping up her housekeeping? And that's it? That's what you've discovered so far?'

'Sshh, Ted. It's a bit more complicated that that actually—'

'And how long have you got left to sort things out, before they haul you back in?'

'Till Saturday.'

'And today is?'

'Tuesday?'

'It's Monday, you eejit. I think you'll be needing a hand then, eh, if you don't even know what day of the week it is? Here, take these.'

206

Israel helped Ted take pints back to the tables.

'So?' said Ted, drinks delivered, sitting down.

'We need to look at this logically,' said the man called Big Red.

'Aye,' added One Brow. 'Why would anyone kidnap him?'

'Because he disturbed them?' said a Billy.

'Wouldn't he just become a liability?' said One Brow.

'Why?'

'Because he knew their identity?'

'Aye, well, there is another possibility,' said another Billy.

'Which is?'

'He was working with them.'

'You think Mr Dixon was involved in a criminal gang run by former paramilitaries?' said Tonky, who was smoking a pipe.

'No. Not really,' said a Billy. 'I'm just thinking out loud here.'

'Well, can you not, it's confusing me,' said Tonky.

Israel was keen to make his own voice heard. 'Erm. If I could just—'

'Wesley knows him, don't you, Wesley?' said Ted.

'Aye, Ted. Saw Mr Dixon on the golf course last week.'

'How'd he seem?'

'He looked rightly.'

'You can't judge a book by its cover.'

'Aye.'

'But a rich man has his problems also,' said Wesley.

Israel thought on that for a moment. He thought about all the rich men he knew. Gloria's father: he certainly had his problems. He was some kind of businessman, import-export. He was divorced from Gloria's mother. When Israel was first getting to know Gloria, her parents were both still living in the house together. Terrible atmosphere. Terrible. It had put him off divorce. Whenever Israel went round her father would be banished to the back room, slumped in front of the TV, eating ready meals. A condemned man. Probably the richest person Israel knew was an old friend from college, Pete; he'd gone into some sort of Internet start-up, crested the wave, and these days Israel could never get him to return his calls, and when he did he wished he hadn't, because he'd usually be on board a private jet on his way to Monte Carlo. Last time Israel had spoken to Pete he was just back from a weekend in Iceland; he'd had a good time. In fact, 'Reykjavik is my new party city,' he'd said. They were maybe drifting apart.

'You know, I think he's done himself in,' said Honky, a man for whom the glass seemed always – metaphorically and literally – half empty. 'Pint anyone?'

'Why would he do himself in?' said Tonky.

'Just because,' said Honky, getting up for the bar.

'I think we need to look at this logically,' said Big Red again.

'Aye,' said Tonky. 'People don't just kill themselves for no good reason.'

'There were always those rumours, mind,' said a Sammy.

'What rumours?' said Israel.

'That he was, you know . . .'

'What?'

'A kiddie fiddler,' called Honky from the bar. 'Pints?'

'Aye!' came a collective response.

'Ach,' said Ted. 'Lot of nonsense. That was because he did the children's parties, just.'

'Right,' said Israel. 'Erm, I wouldn't mind some crisps, actually . . . Tonky?'

'Honky,' said Honky. 'Tayto cheese and onion?'

'Please. I'll have two packets actually, if that's . . .'

'Aye. Lads?'

'Aye,' came the further call.

Israel hadn't eaten a proper meal since . . . Saturday? It had been all crisps and sandwiches. He thought he'd maybe lost a few pounds. He was on the fugitive diet, but he couldn't recommend it. A stomach staple would be easier.

'I think he's just taken hisself off,' said Wesley, who spoke as though he'd recently eaten a large mixed grill which, being a butcher, he probably had.

'Why would he take hisself off?' said Ted.

'To get away.'

'To get away from what though?'

'People do, don't they? Just throw up the head and . . .'

'Aye,' agreed a Sammy. 'What about that fella Stephen, what do you call him, a few years back? Mate of yours, Ted?'

'Who?'

'Stephen Crawford?' said another Sammy.

'Aye. Him. Played for Tumdrum Young Men. He disappeared, didn't he?'

'Ach, no. That was different,' said Ted. 'Sure, he just went down to work at Ballylumford.'

'Aye,' agreed Tonky. 'That's not the same thing at all. He just left town.'

'As good as disappearing,' said One Brow.

'But what about Trevor Mann's sister?' said Barney.

'Maureen?'

'Aye.'

'She ran off to join the Dagenham Girl Pipers,' said Barney.

'Aye, that's right.'

'That was years ago,' said Ted. 'We're not comparing like with like here.'

'We need to look at this logically,' said Big Red.

Israel attempted to bring the conversation to order. 'Why would he have gone off though?'

'Another woman?' suggested a Billy.

'No. He's got Mrs Dixon, hasn't he?' said Barney, smoothing down his comb-over.

'Exactly,' said One Brow.

There was general laughter.

'She's not bad, for her age, but,' said Barney regretfully. He looked like the kind of man who might feel the lack of female company.

'A man's needs are manifold,' said Honky.

'Meaning?' said Ted.

'There's more than one way to skin a cat,' said Honky.

'You think he's run off with another woman? And faked his own kidnapping?' said Ted.

'I saw that on *The Bill* once.'

'Aye, but this is not *The Bill*, is it, Honky? This is Tumdrum.'

'Truth can be stranger than fiction, Ted.'

'Most likely he's away with one of the shop girls,' said a Sammy.

'Mr Dixon?'

'Any of them missing?'

'No.'

'Well then.'

'What about wee Davey?'

'The caretaker.'

'Nah.'

'He's a wee skite, but,' said Barney.

'If he stole a pup on the Saturday, he'd have it sold back to you the Sunday,' said Jimmy Savage elliptically.

'He's hardly up to this, though, is he?'

'People are never what they seem.'

'I think we've got to think about this logically,' said Big Red.

'Right,' said Ted. 'Why would a man disappear?'

'Woman.'

'Mid-life crisis.'

'No, no, I don't think so,' said Israel.

'Why not?' said Ted.

'I don't know, just . . .'

'What would make you disappear then?'

'I wouldn't disappear,' said Israel.

'Well, what are you doing here then?'

'I haven't disappeared. I'm . . . working.'

'Well, maybe Mr Dixon fancied a career change.'

'Mr Dixon? A businessman?' said One Brow.

'Sure, we'd all jump at the chance, wouldn't we?' said Honky. 'To just go . . .'

There was an enthusiastic nodding of heads around the table.

'Eight years to retirement,' said One Brow. 'And counting every day.'

'Ray's ready for you, Ted,' called a barman.

'Lads,' said Ted, excusing himself and getting up.

Israel sat on, finishing off his second packet of crisps.

'Come on then, you big galoot.'

'What?'

'Get up. Come on. Don't hang about.'

Israel swallowed the rest of the crisps and followed Ted, ducking down under the back bar.

'Ted?'

'We're going to see Ray,' said Ted, making his way down a short, dark, piss-stinking corridor, past crates and bottles.

'Who's Ray?'

'Ray.'

'Right. Well, why are we going to see Ray?'

'He's connected.'

'To?'

'The people who might've lifted Mr Dixon.' Ted knocked at a door at the end of the corridor.

'Jesus! What?'

'Sshh. He knows people who know people.'

'Oh, my God.'

The door was unlocked and opened by a vast man in a vast leather car-coat.

'Ray,' said Ted.

'Hello, Ray,' said Israel.

'That's not Ray,' said Ted.

'Oh. Sorry.'

The vast man did not respond.

Ray was presumably the man seated at the table on the far side of the room. He was wearing sunglasses. Which seemed unnecessary: the room was not sunny. In fact the room had no windows. But the lack of light looked as though it might not have bothered Ray: he had a pale, weak face, cracked and streaky with burst blood vessels. He did not say hello. There was no shaking of hands with Ray.

'So, Ted.'

'Ray. Appreciate you coming.'

'OK.'

Ted slipped Ray an envelope of cash.

'I won't count it, Ted.'

'No, it's all there.'

'Ted, what are you doing?' said Israel.

'Ray's been acting on our behalf.'

'What?'

'I've had words,' said Ray.

'What do you mean you've had words?' said Israel.

'He's not been kidnapped.'

'No?' said Ted. 'I didn't think so.'

'Not by any of ours.'

'What do you mean "ours"?' said Israel.

'Shut up, Israel.'

'Our lot,' said Ray.

'Which is?'

'Half of one, and half a dozen of the other,' said Ray, tapping the side of his nose with his finger.

'So?' said Ted.

'We think there's a woman involved.'

'Ah!' said Ted. 'I thought so.'

'And the Dixon boy might be worth talking to.'

'The boy?' said Israel. 'Do they have a son?'

'Aye. Course.'

'He wasn't there today though, at the police press conference.'

'He wouldn't be,' said Ray.

'Why?'

'He's away down in Belfast,' said Ray.

'He'd have been on the radio,' said Ted.

'Why?'

'He's a programme.'

'What sort of programme?'

'Phone-in jobby.'

'So,' said Ray.

'Appreciate it, Ray.'

'Not a problem, Ted.'

'That's us sorted then. Let's go.'

Ted and Israel made their way back into the corridor.

'Who the hell was he?'

'I said, he's someone who knows people.'

'Well, what sort of people?'

'People who know people.'

'Who know people who know people? What is it, infinite regress? What are we talking about?'

'Just.'

'And you were paying money for that sort of information?'

'Aye.'

'So where did you get that from?'

'It's creative accounting. End of the tax year. It's a couple of leads there, well worth it. We'll check out the son tomorrow.'

In the back room some of the men were drifting away.

'Sorry, lads,' said Big Red. 'Need an early night.'

'How's your father?' said a Billy.

'And your mother still working?' said a Sammy.

Which made them laugh.

'All right, fellas.'

'Night.'

'Safe home.'

More drink was provided for the remaining brains trust.

'I don't know how you drink that stuff,' said Israel, as Ted tucked into another Guinness.

'What?'

'It's disgusting. It's like drinking fermented dog juice.'

'Cheers,' said Ted.

'Cheers,' said Israel, rubbing his stomach and belching. He was on lager. 'I thought you were off the drink anyway?'

'Sometimes I'm off; sometimes I'm on.'

'Right.'

'Tonight I'm on.'

It had been a long couple of days, and it turned into an even longer night.

There was a political discussion going on.

Israel decided to keep out of it. His grasp of Northern Irish politics was sketchy, to say the least. He had some idea there'd been a civil war or something similar. The most political he'd ever been was at university, when he briefly joined the Jewish Socialist Society, which he'd only joined because he was, notionally, Jewish, and notionally a socialist. He never went to any of the meetings.

He couldn't remember much of what happened during the rest of the evening, though he did vaguely recall one of the Billys telling him about a cousin of his who was a pastor who operated out of a mission hall in north Belfast and who was caught with two Russian grenades and a pipe bomb on the outskirts of Dungannon, and then another Billy starting in with the old argument that 'Sure, this was a great wee country until all the immigrants started coming in,' and another similar conversation with another Billy which began with the statement, 'At least you knew where you were with the Troubles,' and went downhill from there.

Bruce Springsteen had just kicked in on the jukebox with 'Born in the USA' when Elder appeared at the bar.

'Turn that fucking music off and get out, you cunts!'

Only Ted and Israel were left. Israel was at that drooling, many's-the-slip stage in his drinking, where everything you lift to your mouth does not necessarily reach its destination.

'I am large,' he said to Ted. 'I contain multitudes.'

'Aye, right,' said Ted.

'No sweeter fat than sticks to my own bones.'

'Why don't you join a gym or something?' said Ted.

'Because,' pomped Israel, 'I don't believe . . .' – and he was struggling then – 'I don't believe the body should . . .'

'Once a . . .' began Ted, sighing.

'Catholic?' said Israel.

'No, thanks,' said Ted. 'I've eaten already. Don't worry about it. You're just getting old.'

'I'm not getting old.'

'How old are you?'

'I'm not even thirty.'

'Aye, well, you're getting there. Anyway, I'm away here.'

'Right,' said Israel. 'I'll just get my . . .'

'You're not coming with me.'

'What?'

'You're a flippin' liability, son. I don't want the police dragging me into this far—'

'Far out?'

'Rago of nonsense.'

'Right. So where am I staying? I can't go back to the farm. They'll be . . .'

'You're staying here.'

'Where?'

'Here, the First and Last.'

'Do they have rooms?'

'This is the room.'

'I can't sleep here.'

'You'll be safe here. I'll pick you up at eight, all right?'

'Hold on, Ted!'

But by the time he got to the door Ted had gone, locking the door behind him.

It gave a new meaning to the phrase 'lock-in'.

CHAPTER 14

He seemed to be blind in one eye. And someone had inflated a paper bag inside his head. There was a kind of banging going on somewhere.

Oh, God.

He'd not slept the best – not good at all. At first he couldn't get to sleep, and then when he did he dreamt all night long, terrible tormenting dreams, like something out of a David Lynch film. *Eraserhead* – gave him nightmares for years.

First, he'd dreamt that he was standing alone in a bookshop – the Discount Bookshop at the Lakeside Shopping Centre in Thurrock in Essex, just off the M25 – browsing, having wandered in aimlessly off the street. In the dream no one in the whole world knows that he's there. The phone rings at the back of the shop and the assistant goes to answer it. 'Yes,' the assistant says, 'he's here. I'll just get him for you.' The assistant begins walking towards him. How do they know he's there? Something terrible has happened.

That was bad enough but then he dreamt that he was arriving home at the flat he shared with

Gloria – away from Tumdrum at last. He was walking up the stairs, before the final turn. There was a man asleep on the doorstep. And a slick of blood on the carpet. He rushes into the flat, treading blood into the carpet. Something terrible has happened.

And then finally he dreamt that there was a man standing next to him on the Tube. The man slowly produces a pen and paper from his pocket, and writes down a few words. It's a message for him. He's about to pass it to him. Something terrible has happened.

Half delirious, his head throbbing, he tried to remember where he was. He had no idea. Was he at home with Gloria? No. At the farm? The police station? Rosie's?

No.

He was staring up at flaking yellow plaster, there was beer swilling in his stomach, there was the stench of . . . what was that smell? It was a smell like . . . urinated Marmite.

And something else. He felt underneath the bench, touched something. A big container. Bleach. 'Chunky's Fragranced Channel Cubes – Minimum 200 Yellow Cubes – Specially Formulated for use in URINALS and WASH-ROOMS to combat unpleasant odours.'

Ah, yes. He was in the back room of the First and Last. He was all sweaty. His clothes stank of cigarettes and beer.

He tried to get up but couldn't. He raised

himself on one elbow and looked down at himself. Fully clothed, on a bench, domed belly rising up before him, weary legs down below, and a head that felt like it was on fire.

He heaved himself up onto his feet. As long as he could just keep himself balanced he'd be fine. The First and Last. Oops. Steady. It was like having tides within him. He was at the First and Last because . . .

Oh, God. That's right. When all this was over he was going to need a therapist, or an analyst: Freudian, or maybe Kleinian, or Jungian, or cognitive-behavioural, Gestalt. ECT. And a shower.

There was that knocking. Ted walked in.

'Let's go, you idle rascal.'

Israel was in the van for half an hour, stomach churning, chest heaving, head dozing, before he could find the powers to speak.

'We're in the mobile, Ted.'

'Aye. Well spotted. All that education didn't go to waste then.'

'But—' began Israel. Every time he opened his mouth it was as though he was going to be sick.

Ted had thoughtfully provided him with a plastic bag; 'Just try not to spray, OK?' he said. 'We've not got much time. I'm not pulling over.'

Israel had the bag clutched in both hands.

'The mobile. I thought the police. Had. As their centre of . . .'

'They did.'

'So?'

'D'you want to let the peelers get a hold of the van?'

'No, but. How did you . . . ?'

'I borrowed it back.'

'Oh, no, Ted.'

'No one cleared it with me. As far as I'm concerned the library remains in use.'

'But what if . . .'

'I'll plead ignorance.'

Israel gave a huge soupy belch, groaned, and felt a little better.

There was an answering sound from the back of the van.

'What's that?'

'It's the dog.'

'Ah, Ted, did you have to bring the dog?'

'What have you got against dogs?'

'I haven't got anything against dogs. I just . . . don't like dogs.'

'Why?'

'It's their . . . They bite you.'

'Well, she's not going to bite you.'

'She?'

'It's Mrs Muhammad. My other wee Jack Russell. I had to bring her along, she's pregnant.'

'What?'

'Right, now, shush. You've got to hear this,' said Ted, reaching to switch on the radio in the van.

'No, Ted. I'm really not into breakfast radio.'

'Aye, it's breakfast radio, but not as you know it.'

'I've quite a . . . headache actually, Ted.'

'Aye?'

'You've not got any . . . ?'

'Here.' Ted gave Israel a handful of headache tablets.

'You've come prepared.'

'You're making a habit of it.'

'Am I?'

'Right, yes, and here's water. Now shush. Here we are. It's Robbo.'

'Who Bo?'

'Robbo Dixon. Mr Dixon's son. Listen.'

'I usually listen to the *Today* programme in the mornings.'

'Aye. Well, change'll do you no harm.'

The *Today* programme: God, now he thought about it, that seemed like a lifetime ago, waking up to the *Today* programme back in north London, in his own bed, in his own flat. His mum used to love Rabbi Lionel Blue: 'Good morning, John. Good morning, Jim. And good morning, all of you.' It was luxury, listening to the *Today* programme: like waking up wrapped in a silk kimono and wandering down to the Senior Common Room, with grapefruit and kedgeree for breakfast, laid out on fresh white linen, and a pre-Murdoch copy of *The Times* propped up against a jar of good thick-cut marmalade. That was another life. Not his. Like getting up late, if he had the day off from the bookshop, and lying in bed, reading the *Guardian*, though why he bothered with the *Guardian* he didn't know; it was the principle of the thing, because he already knew the news and he hated all the columnists and never had the time or inclination to read the dull and detailed comment and analysis, and he couldn't afford any of the clothes or the meals or the houses or the holidays or the home furnishings, and was never interested in the features on celebrities or dead people. Or it was like a Saturday morning, down to Borough Market, or Waitrose at least, him and Gloria. Holding hands, fondly squeezing Fair Trade melons, and the most difficult decision they had to make was whether to go for free range, or organic, or both.

Had he actually ever lived that life? Was that his life? Wasn't that someone else's life he was imagining?

Whatever the hell it was they were listening to now, hurtling along in the van, it was not the *Today* programme.

'That,' the man was half shouting, 'is unbelievable!'

'It is,' said the caller. 'It's unbelievable.'

'It. Is. Unbelievable! D'you know that?'

'It is, Robbo, yes. It's unbelievable.'

'D'you know what I think? I think these people . . .' The man's voice was steadily rising, in pitch, tone and volume. 'These people are not yobs! They're not thugs! They're not just low-lifes! D'you know that? These people . . .' His voice couldn't get any higher or harsher now. 'These people . . .' Oh, yes it could. 'Are the scum of the earth!' He said it in a way in which the words tumbled together – scumoftheearth.

'They are,' agreed the caller. 'That's exactly what they are, Robbo. They are the scum of the earth.'

'Caller on line two?'

More random ranting continued for a while and then there was a record – 'It's Raining Men', the Weather Girls – completely unannounced and unexpected, like the Weather Girls had all just wandered into the studio, midrant, and set up and started singing. And then there was another caller. No continuity. No sequence. Then another record: Dexys Midnight Runners. No intro, no explanation, no seamless links. Total chaos. A disabled man ringing in to complain about disabled access. Then Eminem. The whole thing held together only by the raging voice of the presenter.

'How long does this go on for?' said Israel.

'Two hours.'

'He keeps this up for two hours? What, once a week?'

'Five mornings a week, plus the TV.'

'Jesus!'

'Aye, I've heard he's a fan.'

Another caller: someone who'd been robbed.

'So. You were in the town centre there. And these people attacked your son?'

'That's right, Robbo.'

'And they pulled him out of the car?'

'That's right.'

'And they beat him?'

'Yes, that's right, Robbo.'

'About the head?'

'That's right.'

'Well, you know what I think about these people?'

'I do, Robbo.'

'They're not thugs. They're not scum. They're not . . . You know, I can't even find words this morning.'

'They belong behind bars, Robbo, that's where they belong.'

'But sure, you know what the prisons are like these days.'

'They're like hotels, Robbo.'

'That's right, they're like hotels. We need to treat these people the way they deserve to be treated.'

'We do, Robbo.'

'We need to hunt these people down and sort these people out!'

'We do, Robbo, we do. Sure, if I could get my hands on them, I'd—'

'Now you know I can't condone violence on this show.'

'No, I know, Robbo. But they should all be shot, sure.'

'I know, I know. But we can't say that on the show. They won't let us say that.'

'You're only saying what a lot of us is thinking, Robbo.'

'I know, I know.'

'Your programme is brilliant, sure.'

'Well, like you say, I'm only saying what a lot of us are thinking. It's people like you ringing in that make this programme.'

'You're doing a great job, Robbo.'

'Thank you. Caller on line three?'

'I can't listen to any more of this,' said Israel.

'Sshh,' said Ted.

'Robbo, listen, I'm just ringing in here about us older people.'

'How old are you?'

'I'm sixty-three, Robbo.'

'Sixty-three!'

'That's right, Robbo. And I'll be honest with you – I'm fit enough, mind. I worked in the ship-yard twenty-eight years – but the way things are going these days I'm scared to go out at night.'

'You can't walk the street at night because you're scared?'

'That's right, Robbo.'

'Is that really true?'

'It is, Robbo. Wait till I tell you. There's a bunch of young fellas around where I live—'

'Where do you live?'

'I don't want to say, Robbo.'

'Why don't you want to say?'

'In case, you know.'

'What?'

'They might come after me, Robbo.'

'You're too scared to say where you live because you're scared these hoods who are – what? – terrorising your community?'

'That's right, Robbo.'

'Might come after you?'

'That's right.'

'You know, when people hear that they are just going to despair. I mean, what is our society coming to? When a man of your age – not an old man – can't walk the streets at night?'

'I don't know, Robbo. These fellas round and about here, you see, they're shouting abuse at the old people, tearing around on these quad bikes. I've nearly been knocked down meself now a couple of times. It's a disgrace, so it is.'

'You know what I think? About these young people, these hoods that are doing this to our communities, terrorising—'

'That's right, Robbo.'

'—terrorising our communities? These people are scum! That's what they are! They are worthless scum!'

'They're scum, Robbo, so they are.'

'And yet, if we say that, we get these do-gooders come crawling out of the woodwork ringing in here and saying it's not their fault. It's because of the Troubles or some other lot of nonsense. It makes me – I'll be honest with you – it makes me sick. It actually makes me feel physically sick.'

'Exactly, Robbo.'

'D'you know what we should do?'

'No.'

'I'll tell you what I think we should do. I think

we should find these people. I think we should get a hold of these people.'

'They're lower than the low, Robbo.'

'There's no word in the English dictionary that can describe what I feel about these people.'

'That's right, Robbo.'

'They're talking about building a football stadium at the Maze, aren't they?'

'Yes.'

'D'you know what I think? I think we should reopen it. I think we should reopen it and set it up as a boot-camp, you know. Like a detention centre. Somewhere where they know they've been.'

'You should start a campaign, Robbo.'

'Maybe we will. Maybe we'll start a campaign to get the legislation changed. Have them properly punished. Really punished. Because you know what they are, these people?'

'The scum of the earth?' said Israel.

'Exactly!' said Ted.

Israel leant forward and switched off the radio. 'I can't listen to that, Ted.'

'What?'

'That's awful. That's like . . . It's like listening to Adolf Hitler.'

'I don't think so.'

'It is. It's the same principle.'

'No, it's not.'

'Is it like that every day?'

'Of course. That's why people listen.'

'Him shouting and ranting?'

'People love that, sure. He calls a spade a spade.'

'And that's a skill?'

'Aye.'

'Isn't that just a basic command of the English language?'

'Aye, well, you'd have fancy ideas about it, but.'

'The bloke's stark raving mad.'

'He speaks on behalf of a lot of us ordinary people . . .'

'What? I'm an ordinary person, and he doesn't speak on my behalf.'

'I hardly think you count,' said Ted, swinging the mobile library into another lane.

Israel's stomach lurched with the van. They were on a six-lane motorway – twelve all told, six lanes one way, six the other – and it was heavy, heavy traffic, like the North Circular at rush hour.

'Bloody hell, where is this?' said Israel.

'Belfast City,' said Ted, keeping his eyes firmly on the road, 'where the girls are all pretty.'

'This is it?'

'Aye.'

Israel knew Belfast only through television, where it was mostly dark and where there were only men in balaclavas with guns, or boys with scarves tied around their faces throwing bricks, or thick-set men in heavy overcoats doing their piece straight to camera. Israel had expected something spectacularly bad of Belfast, something immense and dramatic and ruinous, but Belfast refused to live up to its image. In reality, Belfast was a bit like Bolton, or Leeds: all the start-ups and ruins of industry; a disused mill, a warehouse, a derelict factory, lowrise industrial estates. Belfast was a big disappointment. For better and for worse, Belfast looked like anywhere else.

They drove through docks, past big new buildings which looked like big new buildings anywhere, and eventually pulled up outside the BBC building, which looked like a miniature version of the BBC at Langham Place in London, though lacking Eric Gill's famous creamy white Portland stone statue of Prospero and Ariel with his penis, which had always fascinated Israel, even as a child, going past on the C2 bus up to Camden. What was it, the BBC's remit? To inform, to educate, and to entertain? It had certainly done it for Israel; that was his sex education.

'So what are we doing?' asked Israel.

'Waiting for Robbo.'

'Can't we just go in and ask if we can talk to him?'

'No, this is a stake-out,' said Ted.

'Oh, come on, Ted. Let's—'

'You think they'd let us just walk into the BBC?'

'Well . . .'

'Ach, wise up. We've time anyway, he's still on the air. And I need to check on the dog.'

Ted brought the dog up to the front of the van, cradling her in his lap.

'Israel, Mrs Muhammad. Mrs Muhammad, Israel Armstrong.'

'She looks tired, Ted.'

'I said, she's pregnant. Right, you just hold her there for a while.'

'Me?'

'Yes.'

'Why?'

'Well, d'you fancy a fry?'

'Where? Is there somewhere about?'

'No. Here.'

'In the van?'

'Yes. Of course.' Ted lifted up the cover on a bench behind the driver's seat. 'We've the wee gas rings and the grill here.'

'Ah. I always wondered what that was in there. I thought it was maybe the first-aid kit.'

'Aye, with a Calor gas stove? What d'you think that was for?'

'Sterilising the needles?'

'Holy God, man.'

Ted got out a carrier bag from one of the van's storage cupboards and produced a wrap of bacon and sausages, some soda farls and some eggs.

It's a truth not perhaps universally acknowledged, but one that will doubtless be easily understood and appreciated, that it's difficult to remain a vegetarian in the confined space of a mobile library when there's the smell of fried bacon and sausages and you haven't eaten a square meal for almost a week. Indeed, Israel found it almost impossible to keep his vegetarian resolve as Ted dished out fried bread, sausages, bacon and egg onto two battered old enamel plates.

Israel missed good home cooking; not that his mother ever did any good home cooking. This was a myth about Jewish mothers, in Israel's experience. He knew a lot of Jewish mothers who liked to eat, but who liked to cook? No. None. Gloria's mother had pretensions as a cook, but her meals were always somehow wrong or inappropriate; they were the meals of a woman going through a divorce. Back home in London with Gloria he used to eat out at least once a week, in cheap Italians, or Indians or Chinese round where they lived, or they would meet up somewhere in town. There was this vegetarian restaurant they liked near Old Street, where you used to get saffron lasagne with pistachio and ginger and it was all scrubbed wooden tables and body-pierced Australian waitresses. He hadn't eaten out much since arriving in Tumdrum, partly because he didn't have the money, and partly because the few restaurants there were tended not to offer much in the way of vegetarian options, unless you were content to have champ with your chips.

'D'you not want your bacon and sausage?' said Ted.

'No. I—' Before Israel had a chance to reconsider, Ted had reached across and taken them.

'Ted!'

'I'm seeing if Mrs Muhammad fancies the

sausage. What's the matter with you anyway, you not like bacon?'

'No, I'm vegetarian,' said Israel, regretfully. 'Remember?'

'I thought you were Jewish,' said Ted, waving the sausage in front of Mrs Muhammad; the dog wolfed it.

'You can be both,' said Israel.

'Ah'm sure.'

Israel ate the scrambled egg and fried bread, washed down with tea.

'God, that's good, Ted.'

'Aye.'

'You know what? I feel a bit better actually.'

'Good feed inside you, does wonders. Take the good o' it while it lasts.'

'It feels a bit like being on holiday.'

'Well, don't get too comfy, we're working here, remember.'

They were parked directly outside the BBC, listening to the end of Robbo's show – street crime, scumoftheearth, car theft, scumoftheearth, dog-fouling, scumoftheearth, litter louts, scumoftheearth – and eventually the whole sorry thing came to an abrupt end, crashing into the Village People, 'YMCA'. Half an hour later a flush-faced man emerged from the building, wearing the traditional Belfast overcoat and clutching carrier bags. He looked as though he'd just eaten a very big breakfast, on top of an earlier breakfast, and had maybe been up all night working his way through some giant Easter eggs. He looked like a boy trapped in a fat man's body.

'That's him!' yelled Ted. 'Quick!'

They jumped down from the van and started running after him.

'Mr Dixon!' said Ted. 'Robbo! Robbo!'

'Hello!' said the man, turning round. 'How ye doin'?'

'Can we have a word with ye?' said Ted.

'If it's an autograph you're after I'll not charge ye.' Robbo laughed.

'No, actually,' said Ted. 'We wanted to ask you about your father.'

'My father?' There was an abrupt change in tone. 'What are yous, reporters?'

'No,' said Israel. 'We're librarians.'

'Very funny,' said Robbo.

'No, really we are,' insisted Israel. 'Look.' He pointed over at the mobile library. 'We're from Tumdrum.'

'Tumdrum? My home town? Is that the old mobile library?'

'Aye,' said Ted. 'Good nick, isn't she?'

'I used to get books out there once every two weeks when I was growing up,' said Robbo. This seemed to confuse him. 'OK,' he said. 'So, have we books overdue, or what?'

'No, we just wanted to ask you a few questions about—'

'Yes?'

'Look, Robbo,' said Ted, grabbing Robbo's

elbow. 'The wee fella here' – he nodded towards Israel – 'It's a long story, but we're just looking for a wee bit of help with a . . . library project he's working on.'

'Yes!' said Israel. 'It's a five-panel touring exhibition about the history of Dixon and Pickering's.'

'Hmm.' You didn't argue with Ted when he had a hold of your elbow. 'Could you just . . . ?' Robbo tried to wriggle free.

'It's very important. If you could just spare us five minutes.'

'I don't know.'

Ted still had a hold of Robbo's elbow.

'We'll buy you a coffee?' said Israel.

'A library project?'

'Yes.'

'I'll tell you what, you get him to leave hold of me, and you make it a hot chocolate and a tray bake, you're on. Five minutes, mind.'

Ted released his grip.

They went into a café just along from the BBC, a place that was trying to be chic, and which was failing miserably: far too much taupe and too many lilies in too-tall vases filled with pebbles, and not enough comfortable seating. It was like an old Eastern European version of Western Europe; it was a simulacrum of cool. Nonetheless, it had got some things right. A waitress with a foreign accent came to take their order and Israel could have kissed her right there and then – she was the most excitingly ethnically diverse individual he'd come across in a long time.

'What can I get you?' she asked.

'Where are you from?' asked Israel.

'I'm from the Czech Republic,' she said, Czechly.

'God. I mean, wow. That's . . . How on earth d'you end up here?'

'I'm a student.'

'Wow. What are you studying?'

'I'd doing my PhD on Seamus Heaney, up at Queen's.'

'Right. Between my finger and my thumb the squat pen rests? I'll dig with it.'

'Just ignore him,' said Ted. 'He doesn't get out much.'

'Great poem,' said Israel.

'Aye, and you'd know, would ye?' said Ted. 'You never been getherin praitas in yer life, man.'

'What?'

'Tubers.'

'Sorry, you lost me, Ted.'

'It's a poem about peat and potatoes, for guidness sake. I'll take a coffee, love.'

'Regular?'

'Cappuccino.'

'And for you?' said the waitress.

'I thought it was about writing?' said Israel.

'It's about potatoes,' said Ted. 'Ask the expert here.'

'Is it about writing?' said Israel.

237

'I think it can be about both,' said the waitress.

'Thank you,' said Israel.

'Coffee?' repeated the waitress.

'Espresso, please,' he said, satisfied.

'And Mr Dixon, what do you think?' she asked. 'Will he have his regular?'

'I would have thought so,' said Israel. 'By the look of it.'

Robbo was busy circulating round the tables, signing autographs. People were coming up to him, offering opinions on his show.

'Great show, Robbo,' they said.

'Thanks.'

'Love it,' said another.

'Hi!' he was saying, and 'Hello!' and 'Great to see you!' and 'Thanks,' 'All right!' and this seemed to go on for an age, but eventually people grew accustomed to having greatness among them and Robbo drifted back to Israel and Ted.

'Belfast,' said Robbo. 'You gotta love it.'

'Sure,' said Israel.

'Great wee city,' said Ted.

'It is,' said Robbo. 'But you know what I think? It's the people who really make it.'

'Scum of the earth,' said Israel.

'Sorry?'

'Nothing.'

'So, gents, now we're here, let's talk,' said Robbo, who was tucking into his luxury hot chocolate with whipped cream, marshmallows and a flake, with a side order of caramel slice. 'Shoot.'

Israel and Ted looked at each other hopefully. They hadn't worked out exactly what it was they wanted to ask.

'Israel?' said Ted.

'Ted?' said Israel.

'Gents? If you're going to ask me a question for your project, ask me a question. Your time's running out.'

'Do you know where your father is, Mr Dixon?' said Ted.

'No! Of course not! If I did, I would have told the police.'

'Are you and your father . . . close?' said Israel.

'No. We had a falling out a few years ago. This has all been covered before, though, in other interviews. It's been in the papers.'

'Yes, of course,' said Israel.

'What sort of project did you say you were working on?'

'It's to do with the history of Dixon and Pickering's.'

'Well, I don't know if I can help you much with that.'

'And . . .' Israel had to think. 'People who work in family businesses.'

'Ah! I see.'

'So,' continued Israel, 'how did you end up down here, in Belfast?'

'I had to get away, because of the business.'

'Really?'

'Well, you're from Tumdrum, you know the store?'

'Yes.'

'Well, you know the score. He had this whole thing, you know, my father, about me, the only son, taking on the family business.'

'I see.'

'Lot of pressure, you know, because Dixon and Pickering's was—'

'Formed in 1906 when Mr Dixon, the haberdasher, inherited money from a distant relative sent out to seek his fortune in New South Wales,' said Israel.

'How do you know that?'

'It's a part of my project.'

'Right. OK. And anyway, there was this whole family thing, and I wasn't interested.'

'I see.'

'Never was. Always wanted to do my own thing.'

Robbo was dunking his marshmallows, self-reflectively, into his hot chocolate, like Narcissus with his pool before him.

'So, what?' asked Israel. 'Was it passed on, the business, on to your sisters?'

'No. No. My dad's hung on in there. He wanted a man at the helm, you know, which is crazy, because it was always my mother who was the real brains behind the business.'

'As is traditional,' said Israel.

'Yes,' said Robbo. 'She had a real flair. Her mother was French, you know. She always oversaw the range of furnishings stocked at the shop. She's got a real eye, you know: she travels to all the trade shows over in Birmingham, and in Milan, and in Germany.'

'I don't want to be personal,' said Ted, who was getting fed up with Israel's low-level-chat approach to interviewing informants, 'but do you know anything about any other women in your father's life?'

'I'm not answering that!'

'No,' said Israel. 'No, of course not. My colleague here was just . . . Difficult living with those sorts of family tensions,' Israel went on, thinking about Gloria's family, and his own. 'You know, with your sisters, and your parents.'

'Aye, well. There's always a lot of strains, I think, running your own business. I mean, I'm basically my own business now, if you see what I mean. My own brand.'

'Right,' said Israel with distaste.

'And you have to work hard at it. My parents worked hard at it. The only times they were ever really relaxed and happy was when we were on holiday in Donegal.'

'Ah,' said Ted fondly. 'Whereabouts did ye go?'

'Inishowen peninsula?' said Robbo.

Ted nodded.

'But mostly it was around Lough Swilly. D'you know it?'

'A wee bit.'

'Rathmullan.'

'Ach, beautiful.'

Robbo drank down the rest of his hot chocolate in one considerable gulp.

'Listen, boys, I would love to chat more about Donegal and about the history of Dixon and Pickering's but I don't really think I can tell you anything else you wouldn't be able to discover elsewhere.'

'Oh, I don't know,' said Israel.

'The police are coming down this afternoon, actually, from Tumdrum, to talk to me about this business with my father and the store, so, you know, it's going to be a long day.'

'Ah, yes,' said Israel, 'terrible business. I hope they catch whoever's responsible.'

'The PSNI?' said Robbo. 'I doubt it.'

'Right, well, thanks for your time,' said Israel.

'Didn't get very far there then, did we?' said Israel, when they were back in the mobile.

'What do you mean we didn't get far? I've got it. I know where to find Mr Dixon!' said Ted. 'Brilliant work by you there!'

'What?'

'That softly-softly approach. Brilliant!'

'Was it?'

'Aye, just gaining his trust there, drawing the information out of him.'

'Well, I . . .'

'Come on then.'

Ted started up the van.

There was a uniformed policeman walking past

the BBC. He was looking towards the van. He was talking into his walkie-talkie.

'Israel, we need to get out of here!' said Ted, throwing the van into reverse. 'Quick! Get your head down.'

Ted pulled away and drove fast up and down the tight narrow streets surrounding the BBC.

'Are we all right?' said Israel.

'I don't know,' said Ted. 'We're going to have to take the scenic route.'

'Ted?'

'Yes?'

'The dog's making a funny noise in the back.'

'What?'

'In the back there, the dog, it's sort of panting and . . .'

'All right, go and have a look.'

Israel crawled on his hands and knees towards the back of the van, where Ted had wedged the dog basket between Fiction and Reference. He peered in.

'I think we've got an emergency here, Ted.'

The pregnant dog in the back of the van was heaving and yelping and a tiny sac of something – something horrible – was protruding from her.

'Something's coming out here, Ted!'

'Oh, Jesus. You're joking?'

'No.'

'Right, you're the midwife.'

'What?'

'The sausage must have upset her. She's not due till next week, sure.'

'What? She's not actually going to . . . Is she?'

'Mrs McCready's son up at the vet's checked her. He thought probably around next Tuesday.'

'Right, but Ted?'

'I've the birthing box and the heater at home all ready for Tuesday.'

'But it's not Tuesday, Ted, it's now.'

Ted shook his head, looking for an explanation.

'Right, I'm holding you responsible for this, Israel, all right? You're going to have to follow my—'

'Oh God, oh God, oh God!'

'What? In the name of Jesus!' Ted swerved, trying to look round.

'Ted, I think it's coming! What am I supposed to do? Do you leave it to it?'

Israel was trying not to be sick, holding on to a tiny sac that had spurted out of Mrs Muhammad, who was looking at him with wide, terrified eyes.

'Oh, God! It's out, Ted. No, it's in!'

'Ach, wise up. Have you never done lambing?'

'I live in north London!'

'Aye, well that's your excuse for everything. Right, first, just calm down. Is it breathing?'

'What?'

'The pup, man.'

'I don't know.'

'Feel it.'

'Yes! Yes! Thank God! It's breathing.'

'Good. I've whacked the heating up here, we need to keep them warm. Take my coat here as well. Come on!'

Israel wanted to cry but no tears came.

He grabbed Ted's coat and crouched back down awkwardly over the dog, and held on gently to the tiny sac which was oozing over his hands and his trousers. The stacks of books observed and judged him silently, his total lack of knowledge of the most basic of animal functions.

Meanwhile, Ted was gunning the van through the streets of Belfast.

'Ted! Actually, I really don't think I can do this. The little dog's all hot and it's not moving, Ted. I think there's something wrong. I'm going to be sick.'

'You're not going to be sick.'

'I am!'

'Wise up, boy . . .'

'TED!'

Mrs Muhammad's licks had opened up the sac and the tiny puppy squeezed blindly out and onto Israel's lap, slimy and warm. Israel instinctively tucked it into the folds of his jacket.

'He's out! Ted! He's out!'

'Don't forget to cut the cord!' said Ted. 'Don't just leave him dangling there!'

'What? I don't know what you're talking about. Ted! Pull over!'

'I'm not pulling over. We've got to get out of Belfast before the PSNI set up any roadblocks.'

'Roadblocks!'

'You'll have to use dental floss to tie it off. I use dental floss at home. Have you any dental floss?'

'Ted! DO I LOOK LIKE I HAVE A TOILETRY BAG IN MY POSSESSION?'

'All right, I've mine somewhere. It's in the wee cupboard there.'

Israel found the bag, got the dental floss.

'Tie it off!' shouted Ted. 'Don't tear it! Tie it! Careful. If you do it wrong the pup gets a hernia, or bleeds to death.'

'I am being careful! Can't you slow down a bit?'

'No!'

As soon as Israel had tied off the umbilical cord and wrapped up the puppy Mrs Muhammad heaved and yelped and another sac appeared. The van's blower was on full, there was a bloody mess on the floor and the puppies kept on coming.

As they were heading out of Belfast, Mrs Muhammad's fourth and last puppy emerged – this one without a sac. Israel, fumbling, tucked the fourth bundle into his jacket while – unbelievably – Mrs Muhammad began to lick and chew the mass of bloody tissue she had deposited on the floor of the van.

'Oh, God, Ted. It's disgusting. She's . . .'

'What?'

'She's eating all that . . . stuff.'

'That'll be her then. So what is it, four?'

'Yes, four.'

'All live?'

'Yes.'

'Got 'em suckling?'

'Erm. Yuck. Yes.'

Israel sat cradling the dog and her pups, wrapped in Ted's coat, close up to the van's fan heater.

'So? We lost the police?'

'I think so.'

'And where are we going?'

'Where do you think?'

'I have no idea. I don't even know what day of the week it is.'

'It's Tuesday and we're going to find Mr Dixon.'

'Yeah, right. And where is he?'

'Well, think, where would you go, if you had to disappear?'

'Home?'

'Home? You eejit. You escape *from* home. You don't escape to it. Honest, one day I'm going to take my boot and kick you up the erse so hard you'll not come back.'

'Not home?'

'You don't go home to escape. You go to the place where once you were happy.'

'Where's that?'

'For most people in Northern Ireland? Donegal. That's the teat. That's where we go when the going

247

gets tough. It's here but not here, if you catch my drift.'

'I think so,' said Israel. 'Yep. I think I know exactly what you mean.'

CHAPTER 15

Israel and Ted drove for most of the rest of the day in the mobile library, Israel tending to the puppies and reading the map – 'Were you born stupit?' Ted yelling, after every wrong turn. They tried to keep off the major roads, in order to avoid the police, and they took a circuitous route, skirting their way around the coast up to Coleraine, then over to Magilligan Point, where they caught a ferry across to Greencastle, and then down to Londonderry, and up again to Buncrana.

'Have we crossed the border?' Israel kept asking.

'A long time ago,' said Ted.

'And how much further?' Israel kept asking.

'Not far now. Let's have some music,' said Ted, 'soothe the dogs.'

'All right,' said Israel. 'As long as it's not that . . .'

'I've the cassette here somewhere,' said Ted.

'As long as it's not that . . .'

'Ah! Here we are. The Field Marshal Montgomery.'

'Pipe band,' said Israel.

'Champion of Champions, so they were.'

If Israel had heard Ted's cassette of the Field

Marshal Montgomery Champion of Champions pipe band once, he'd heard it a thousand times, and it was not music you warmed to; it was like having someone beating you with sticks. Or cabers.

'Campbeltown Loch,' shouted Ted, as the skirling started up. 'Och aye, the noo!'

'Are you sure he's going to be there?' said Israel.

'Who?'

'Mr Dixon.'

'I'm sure.'

'Why are you sure?'

'Look, can you remember the periodic table?' said Ted.

'What?'

'From school. Can you remember the periodic table?'

'Erm . . .'

'No. Fine. Your times tables?'

'Yes, of course.'

'Seven eights then?'

'I don't know what seven eights are, Ted.'

'Well.'

'What is your point exactly?'

'Second Law of Thermodynamics?'

'All right, all right. Your point?'

'People can't remember, even basic facts. OK?'

'Yeah.'

'We all have to be reminded. Everyone's the same. So if Mr Dixon's away, he's gone into hiding or whatever, then the chances are he's gone somewhere where he can remember what it was like to be himself.'

'I hope you're right, Ted.'

'Well, if I'm wrong, it's Plan B.'

'What's Plan B?'

Ted just looked at Israel.

'Oh.'

When they got to Buncrana they'd missed the last ferry across Lough Swilly to Rathmullan. It was a long drive round without it.

'So now what?' said Israel.

'We'll wait till morning now,' said Ted. 'Element of surprise still with us.'

'Erm. OK. And now?'

'We'll go see an old friend of mine. We need someone to mind the pups for us.'

'You know someone here, in Buncrana?' It seemed to Israel like claiming to know someone in Timbuktu.

'Yes. He's an old surfing friend.'

'Surfing?'

'Aye. Have you heard of that over in England?'

'Of course . . . So, what, you met him on the Internet?'

'No, surfing, you fool, with surfboards.'

'You're a surfer?'

'Used to be. Haven't been out in a while, but.'

'You're having me on?'

'No. I took it up years ago. When I was in Australia.'

'What were you doing there?'

'Another time. How're the pups?'

'They're fine.'

They drove into the centre of Buncrana and pulled up outside a shop called Swilly's.

Swilly's called itself a Sports, Leisure and Gaming Centre, but basically it was a headshop: it had psychedelic T-shirts and lava lamps displayed in the window, and imitation firearms, and knives, and herbal cigarettes, and AC/DC posters, plus wet-suits and surfboards, and Frisbees, and novelty bikinis, and guitars, and sew-on heavy metal badges; if you were about fourteen years old and you were living in Buncrana, then Swilly's probably seemed to you about the coolest place on earth; then again, it wasn't facing a lot of competition. At five thirty on an April evening downtown Buncrana was absolutely deserted. There was a shop opposite Swilly's called Nice Things, which was open but empty; not just empty of customers but actually empty of anything. And next to Swilly's was 'Pat's Manicure and Footcare', which advertised its services as 'Manicure, Polish, Acrylics, Corns, Callouses, And Verucas'; it was not immediately clear whether the few tattered scraps displayed in transparent pouches and stuck to the window were in fact flesh or plastic.

Swilly's was shut, but Ted banged on the door until eventually a man with a vast white moustache and cropped hair emerged from out back.

He was smiling broadly when he unbolted the door and opened up. He had gold front teeth.

'Ted!' he said. 'Where you been, man?' Israel had never before heard an Irish/Californian accent: it was swollen and sweet and guttural, like a raisin in peat.

'Here and there,' said Ted.

'It's good to see you. You're looking great!'

He hugged Ted, and Ted hugged him back, without embarrassment or hesitation; Israel hadn't had Ted down as a hugger.

'So who's this guy?'

'He's a friend. Israel, this is Tommy. Tommy, Israel.'

'Hi,' said Israel.

'Good to meet you, man.'

'We need a favour, Tommy.'

'Sure, Ted. It's legit?'

'Absolutely, Tommy; those days are over. We just need a place to stay the night.'

'That's not a favour, that's a pleasure, Ted. Come on in.'

'And somewhere to park the van? Out of the way?'

'No problem.'

'Ah,' added Ted, 'and someone to look after a few puppies for us?'

As if on cue, a big curly-haired mongrel came lolloping through the shop towards them.

'You came to the right place, my old friend. The more the merrier.'

Israel, Ted, Mrs Muhammad and the puppies were safely installed in the back of Swilly's headshop, where Tommy appeared to live in squalor. The place was not merely dirty, it was inexplicably dirty: a thick grease on top of the kitchen cupboards; slime on the dish-rack, and what appeared to be acid stains on the lino; the walls sticky with nicotine. The toilet seat in the bathroom was encrusted and its plastic mouldings rotting; a couple of old towels, furry and grey with dirt, hung from grey plastic loops coming away from the wall. And everywhere there were books and records, stacked in milk-crates and in cardboard boxes, piled on every surface. Israel couldn't help but think that unless he got his life sorted out this was perhaps where he was heading.

Tommy prepared white bread and paste sandwiches and a plate of luncheon meat and what he called a 'Tropicana Salad' – some on-the-turn cottage cheese and pineapple chunks – and they drank beer out of polystyrene beakers. There was a cardboard box and a convector heater for the puppies. Van Morrison was playing loudly in the background, bellowing, 'Gloria, G-L-O-R-I-A.'

'Van Morrison was from over here, wasn't he?' said Israel, delighted to be free of the bagpipes.

Ted and Tommy looked at each other and laughed.

'Aye,' said Ted.

'So I believe,' said Tommy.

'What's funny?' asked Israel.

'Tommy here used to play guitar with Van.'

'Right, sure he did.'

'He did.'

'And you're also best friends with Ozzy Osbourne, I suppose.'

'No,' said Tommy. 'But I once met Johnny Cash.'

'Did you?'

'I did.'

'That's . . .'

'What?'

'Incredible?'

'It's also true.'

'He thinks we're all up to nothing over here, Tommy.'

'Ah, a real-life colonial Englishman!'

'No,' said Israel indignantly. 'I am not!'

'You still playing?' asked Ted.

'Not really,' said Tommy. 'Don't get the time, you know. But I tell you what I haven't given up, Ted.'

'What?'

'I've a little of the auld shamrock tea here, if you know what I mean.'

Ted looked shyly at Israel. 'I don't know, Tommy. I've the boy to think about here. We've had a big day today, and it's a big day tomorrow.'

'Shamrock tea?' said Israel.

'You want some?' said Tommy.

'Erm. What does it—'

Tommy winked at him. 'Very refreshing,' he said.

'Oh, right, I get it!'

'You'd take some?'

'Erm . . .'

'You're not of the temperance inclination?'

'No. I . . .'

'I've vodka, if you'd rather. Or I can go and get some—'

'Erm. No, not at the moment. I'm fine, thanks,' said Israel.

'Ted? For old times' sake?'

Israel excused himself and asked if he could use the phone, which was in the shop, and he rang through to the Devines back in Tumdrum. He wanted to see if the police had been looking for him.

They had. The mobile library was featuring quite prominently on local radio and television news; the Chartered Institute of Library and Information Professionals would be delighted. He was expecting George to be furious, but she wasn't. She said she had some bad news for him. He thought maybe that she meant that they were throwing him out of the house, but it wasn't that.

His grandmother had died. She'd died yesterday. Israel's mother had been trying to get in touch with him. It meant he'd have missed the funeral, which would have been today, in accordance with tradition. She'd been taken into hospital, and that was it.

'I'm sorry, Armstrong,' said George.

'Yeah,' said Israel. 'Thanks.'

He was stunned. He walked out of the shop and through the streets of Buncrana, past the kebab shops and amusement arcades, through the usual paper litter and dreck, and down to the lough, which had the view of the paintings that everyone in Northern Ireland seemed to have somewhere in their house: a generic picture of mountains, water, and sky.

So, that was it, his last grandparent gone. His childhood finally over. And here he was, far from home.

He tried to remember good things about his grandmother, but they kept turning to bad. He tried to screen memories in his mind, like he was watching a series of lantern-slides, or a home video, but it didn't work, the mechanism was faulty. He remembered that when he was seven years old she'd bought him a violin, because when you're seven you have to learn the violin. But he couldn't picture the violin, and he couldn't remember if in fact it was his other grandmother, his father's mother, who'd bought it. And besides, he never learned the violin; he lacked the application. He thought about her speaking Yiddish, but he couldn't remember any actual phrases or sentences, just words – *shlump* and *schlep* and *shlemiel* – so it was as if the language itself had packed up in a hurry and left, leaving behind just a few useless ornaments and a couple of bits of unmanageable old furniture. He tried to remember going to synagogue with her as a child, and all he could remember was her giving him liquorice allsorts to keep him quiet, but then he thought that maybe that had been when he'd gone to church with his father, and not with her at all.

And then he thought about being a Jew, how he was really only Jewish in the same way his friends were Church of England: the bar mitzvah, and the occasional service, the odd festival, Hanukkah plus Christmas, a vague sense of being on the side of the good guys rather than the bad. But nothing else; nothing more; if there was anything more. One of his great-grandfathers had been a rabbi, but that was a long time ago and in another country long before Israel was born, and he knew virtually nothing about the rest of his family history; it had never interested him. It didn't seem like history; it was just life. When they were all still alive, what was the point of asking his grandparents about the past? And anyway both his grandparents, his mother's parents, he'd always thought of as English, Protestant almost – more English than the English, in fact, marmalade and net curtains, and milky white tea in a cup and a saucer – although he knew that his grandmother's family was Romanian, and his grandfather's had been from Russia, but they'd been living in England long before the 1930s, long before being Jewish became difficult or a problem. Most of what Israel knew about the Holocaust had come from Art Spiegelman and reading Primo Levi; he was Jewish, but he had no real experience of *being* a Jew; he thought of being Jewish simply as being human, of being who he was. And yet, really, who was he?

Obviously this was not a good or helpful question at the end of what was without a doubt the worst day of the worst week of his life, and yet even this terrible day somehow didn't seem real to him, was not something he could claim definitively for his own. It almost didn't seem to have happened to him. Already it was as if it happened to someone else. And if he was honest what was upsetting about his grandmother's death was not her death as such, but his deep blankness about it. Even his grief seemed second-hand.

He found himself absentimindedly throwing stones into the water.

And that night, lying on the Z-bed at the back of Swilly's, the puppies in their box suckling their mother close by him, he sobbed and sobbed, his chest heaving, and when he woke in the morning his clothes still smelt of beer and cigarettes, and Ted smelt of dope.

Neither of them ate breakfast. Tommy had no food in. They left him in charge of the puppies and drove down to the little quay to catch the early morning ferry over to Rathmullan. While they sat waiting, Israel told Ted about his grandmother.

'Mmm.' Ted shook his head. 'That's not good. I'm sorry to hear that. You have my condolences, of course. You all right?'

'Yeah, I'm fine.'

'You sure?'

'Yeah.'

'You're not going to start howling and wailing? Isn't that what you do?'

'What?'

'Jewish people? Don't they—'

'No. I'm not going to be howling and wailing.'

'Good. Can't be doing with howling and wailing this time in the morning.'

'No.'

They both stared out at the pale, misty sky – like a great blanket, the lough and the mountains laid out carelessly upon it, like yesterday's clothes for the morning.

'I remember when my father died,' said Ted. 'First dead body I ever saw. I was – what? – fifteen, I suppose, just left school. My father was working with this fella, Roy, a builder. My father was like a builder's mate – you know what that is?'

Israel nodded.

'Well, he used to take me along with him some-times, give him a hand, like. It was a house up in east Belfast. I was downstairs, fetching up some bonding. And I heard this thud upstairs, you know.' Ted's voice grew thicker and slower as he spoke. 'I thought at first it was a bag of Carlite Finish. But I went up there, calling out for my da, and there was no reply, and I went into the room, and I was looking at the wall, at the first coat of bonding, which was setting, and I couldn't see him.' Ted cleared his throat. 'He was on the floor. His face was completely white. White with dust – you know, the bonding. I didn't know what to do. You don't. Fifteen.'

'That's terrible.'

'Yeah. And d'you know what I can remember most clearly? The bonding on the wall, which was all scarred, like rivers, or like veins. I can still see it, exactly what it was like. And that was – what? – best part of forty years ago.'

'That's awful.'

'Yeah. Well. You never forget.' Ted nodded behind him. 'I'm not the best person to talk to, probably, when someone's died. But I'll tell you what I do know. You see all those?'

'What?'

'The books.'

'Yep.'

'They'll be no good to you at all, I'm afraid. You can't learn how to grieve from a book. Like you can't learn to deliver a puppy from a book. You just have to do it. That's the only way you learn, in the end. For better or for worse. You did a good job yesterday.'

'Thanks, Ted.'

'That's all right. I wouldn't want to meet you if I was a pregnant woman, mind.'

The ferry arrived and they sailed across.

'This is beautiful,' said Israel.

'It's Lough Swilly,' said Ted. 'You can start with the hotel, OK? I'll take the B&Bs. Let's go and find this bastard.'

Ted drove Israel through Rathmullan and

dropped him off outside the entrance to a grand country house hotel.

It was early morning in the hotel dining room, and sun was streaming in through the vast picture windows. Israel wandered nonchalantly in, doing his best to look as though he belonged, like he'd just come down to breakfast: smart casual, hung over.

The room was busy with couples, mostly elderly, a grand piano forlorn and threatening in the corner. Diners queued along one side of the room by long tables set with vast metal containers of sausages and bacon, liquidy tomatoes and hard, rubbery scrambled eggs, which glistened under harsh bright lights. There were also vast bowls of fruit salad and muesli.

The bacon and sausage looked pretty good. Israel thought he should maybe take at least one sausage and a couple of rashers of bacon, so as not to draw attention to himself. Then he settled down at a corner table to see if Ted was right, and Mr Dixon had returned to some great good place.

He'd seen a lot of photos of Mr Dixon and he knew exactly what he was looking for: the bland face of a manager; the face of an everyman and a no one. He scanned the room: it could have been any of them. *He* could have been any of them.

Then suddenly, coming into the dining room, he saw someone he recognised – not Mr Dixon, but his accomplice.

There she was: Mrs Dixon, the woman who had

wept for the cameras and given moving testimony for local television and radio. Accompanied by her husband.

Israel wiped his mouth with his napkin. His mouth was dry. He allowed them to get their breakfast first – a full fry for Mr Dixon and a fruit salad for Mrs Dixon.

'Excuse me?' he said, as he approached their table once they were settled. 'I wonder if you'd mind if I—'

'Ah!' exclaimed Mrs Dixon, a grapefruit segment and a piece of glacé cherry midway to her mouth.

The diners at the next table glanced across. Israel smiled at them.

'Mrs Dixon,' said Israel. 'And Mr Dixon.'

'Who the hell are you?' said Mr Dixon, under his breath.

'He's the . . . librarian,' said Mrs Dixon.

'The what?'

'The librarian from the mobile library.'

'Can we help you, sir?' said Mr Dixon. 'Are you collecting library books?'

'No.'

'Well, what are you doing here?'

'I was going to ask you the same question actually,' said Israel. 'So,' he said, 'do you want to tell me all about it?'

'About what? I don't know what you're talking about,' said Mrs Dixon.

'I think you do,' said Israel. 'Here you are,

husband and wife. Mrs Dixon with her loving husband, who only forty-eight hours ago you were telling police you feared was dead.'

'Ah. Yes. I . . .'

'She found me,' said Mr Dixon.

'Clearly,' said Israel.

'We were just going to the police,' said Mrs Dixon.

'But you were having your breakfast first?'

'Yes,' said Mrs Dixon.

'Fine. Well, while you're having breakfast, can you just explain to me why you stole the money from your own business, faked your own disappearance, and nearly had me put away?'

A waiter approached the table.

'Is everything satisfactory?' He looked at Israel suspiciously.

'Yes, thank you,' said Mr Dixon.

'I'm just joining my friends here for breakfast,' said Israel.

'By all means. What room number, sir?'

'Erm.'

'It's all right. You can add his bill to ours,' said Mr Dixon.

'Very well.' The waiter turned to walk away.

'Thanks very much,' said Israel. 'In that case, excuse me, waiter?'

'Sir?' The waiter turned back.

'I wonder if I could trouble you for some more toast, maybe some croissants, pastries, and a pot of strong coffee?'

'Certainly, sir.'

'So, here we all are. First things first: the money. Why would you steal your own money?'

'I needed the money,' said Mrs Dixon.

'For what, exactly?'

'Investments.'

'I see,' said Israel.

'Not my own investments. I have these investment clubs.'

'Yes.'

'I needed some sort of challenge of my own, you see,' Mrs Dixon explained. 'I was always very interested in business, but I was never able to exercise what I felt were my talents.'

'But the investment clubs have hardly displayed your talents?'

'We lost a lot on our technology shares, and then there was a cash-flow problem . . .'

'So you owed them money, the investors?'

'Yes.'

'How much?'

'A lot.'

'What? The amount you stole from Dixon and Pickering's?'

'Yes.'

'How many of these investment clubs did you have going?'

'About a dozen.'

'A dozen? And you weren't profiting from any of them?'

'No. They're about women empowering women to—'

'Rip each other off?'

'No!'

Israel's croissants and coffee arrived. At last, a continental breakfast. He was going to savour this. But first he had to clear things up with the Dixons.

'So, anyway, what about Mr Dixon faking his disappearance? What was the point of that exactly?'

'Well, sir, like my wife I'm afraid I feel I may have missed my vocation in life.'

'Which was magic?'

'Correct.'

'I spoke to Walter Wilson.'

'Ah. Yes. Fine magician.'

'He doesn't speak very highly of you.'

'No? Well, we've had our differences. I don't think he ever understood my . . . ambitions.'

'Which were what?'

'To become a professional magician.'

'Well, what I don't understand is why couldn't you just have retired and done that?'

'Dixon and Pickering's is a family business. You can't retire from the family business.'

'Yes, you can.'

'If you have a son to take it on perhaps.'

'Ah, and you don't?'

'That's correct.'

'You have a very angry son who's not interested in the family business.'

'Yes. So I'm afraid in order to pursue my dream

it was necessary for me to . . . disappear. And start again.'

Israel was eyeing a croissant.

'I don't expect you to understand that,' said Mr Dixon. 'You're too young.'

'Well . . . I think I might have an idea actually. But I'm sure the police will understand perfectly.'

'Yes, I wonder if we might be able to come to an accommodation on that issue?'

'Sorry?'

'Fortunately, we are in a position to be able to offer you a sum of money, if—'

'Oh, no,' said Israel. 'I might be a lot of things, but I'm not crooked.'

'Neither are we, Mr Armstrong.'

'We're not criminals,' said Mrs Dixon.

'We didn't mean to cause all this trouble,' said Mr Dixon. 'We're just—'

'Unhappy,' she said.

'Actually' said Israel, 'I need to consult with my colleague.'

He went to ring Ted from the hotel lobby: there was no way the Dixons could get out of the dining room without passing him. There was only the one exit.

Ted was cock-a-hoop – 'Nailed 'em!' he yelled down the phone – and told Israel to keep them there, and, whatever he did, not to let them out of his sight, and he'd get there with the police as quickly as possible.

Israel walked back into the dining room.

'Sir?' said the waiter, as he emerged through the double doors.

'Yes?'

'Your bill, sir?'

'Sorry?'

'Your parents have already checked out, sir.'

'What? But—'

'They left through the patio doors, sir, out through the garden. They said you would take care of the bill.'

'But I don't have any . . .' Israel patted his pockets.

'If there's a problem with the bill, sir, we simply call the police.'

'Oh, no. No.'

'And they left this for you, sir.'

It was a cheque. For £100,000.

CHAPTER 16

He could see her now, Gloria. On the Heathrow Express – well worth the few pounds more. He could see her looking out of the window, at the city petering away, staring up at the sky, at the planes arriving and escaping. Cup of coffee from the concourse. Business lounge? He'd never been in the business lounge. He couldn't even begin to imagine the business lounge.

Ted was dropping him off at Belfast City Airport. They'd spent the past couple of days in Tumdrum, being interviewed by the police. Israel had had his clothes returned, and his phone, the *LRB*. Mr and Mrs Dixon seemed to have disappeared. All ports and airports had been alerted. Back at the farm, Brownie's fish were dead; George was raging. Linda had arranged for a disciplinary meeting of the Mobile Library Steering Committee. Rosie wasn't returning his calls. Veronica had the full inside story for next week's *Impartial Recorder*.

'Were you ever married, Ted?' said Israel, as they came through Belfast.

'I was.'

'But you're not any more?'

'No.'

'Were you divorced, or . . .'

'I'm not in the habit of discussing my private life with colleagues.'

'OK. Fine.'

'I don't wish you to raise the matter again.'

'Sure. Sorry.'

'Why? Were you ever married?'

'No! Of course not. I'm not even thirty.'

'Some men are married and remarried by the time they're thirty.'

'I suppose, yes.'

'Well, you've some catching up to do then, haven't ye? You'd best get yer skates on, or you'll end up with the bachelor's wife.'

'The what?'

'The bachelor's wife.'

'Which is?'

'The wife you imagine.'

Israel had asked Gloria to marry him, actually. A couple of years ago. She'd just laughed. And then he'd asked her again. And again. And again. She said she wasn't ready for marriage. She said she was just getting going at work. He wasn't quite sure how, but somehow they'd managed to stay together, more like brother and sister than . . . Well. He couldn't imagine not being with her. He was going to see how the weekend went, and then maybe . . .

'She's not over for long then, your young lady?' said Ted, as they drove past the Harland and Wolff shipyard.

'No. No. She's got to get back to work for Monday.'

'Aye, right. Hard enough life.'

'Yeah, I suppose.'

'Wouldn't fancy it meself.'

'No.'

'You know when I was young—'

'No. In the 1920s?'

'No. You could breed a few dogs, or pigeons, get a bit of a living: fishing in the spring, bit of building work, apple picking later in the year, and that was you. Your own man. Difficult now just to cover your costs.'

'Yes,' agreed Israel. 'What are you going to do with the puppies, Ted?'

'I'm keeping them for spare parts.'

'You're joking?'

'Of course I'm joking, you eejit. I'm selling them, what did you think? Why? D'you want a puppy?'

'God! No . . . I don't think so.'

'Sure? I'll do you two for one.'

'No, it's all right. Gloria doesn't like dogs.'

The signs welcomed them to Belfast City Airport.

'Well, here we are. Give you a wee break just.'

'Yeah. I need some time to . . .'

'And you're spending the night in Belfast and then bringing her up tomorrow?'

'Yeah. That's the plan.'

'So you're taking her up to the Causeway?'

'Well, I wasn't sure, I don't know if it'd really be her sort of thing.'

'What's her sort of thing?'

'I don't know. She's more . . .'

'What about the Carrick-a-Rede rope bridge?'

'No. I don't think that's quite . . .'

'Everybody loves that. Bushmills? The distillery?'

'Er . . .'

'Ballycastle. Has the market.'

'I'm still thinking, actually, Ted. I haven't quite firmed up the old itinerary yet. We're going to have a lot to . . . you know.'

'Aye, well, if you're looking for ideas.'

'Thanks, Ted. That's—'

'There's always Portrush, if she fancies the bright lights. She'd maybe enjoy that, you know, being from London.'

'Yeah . . .'

'I tell you what I'd do. I'd go for the full works: Ulster fry; up to the Causeway; Carrick-a-Rede; sticky bun in Portstewart; fish supper in Portrush. Get her warmed up. Pop the question.'

'Right. Thanks for that, Ted.'

Ted pulled over into the drop-off area. Israel went to get out of the van.

'Straighten yerself up then.'

'What?'

'Don't be slouching. Look at ye. You're all

hunched over. You should be wearing a suit and a tie to meet your girlfriend.'

Israel had borrowed more of Brownie's clothes: a hoodie, low-slung jeans, the Converse trainers.

'I'd hardly be putting on a suit and a tie to meet my girlfriend, Ted.'

'Aye, well you're not going to get far in life looking like that, all dishelvelled.'

'Dishevelled?'

'Aye. Lean over.'

Israel leant towards Ted.

'And breathe.'

Israel breathed out.

'Aye. Thought so. You've breath like a slurry tank. You know, the tragedy of it is, Israel, for someone as highly educated as yourself, you've not a clue.'

'OK, Ted. Thanks.'

'And cheer up! You've a face'd turn milk sour.'

'All right, thanks, got to dash. Bye!'

The plane was delayed.

At first it was on time, 9.05. Then expected 10.00. Then expected 10.15. 10.45.

'Passengers on BMI flight BD96 to Heathrow, please be advised that the new time of departure for this flight is 11.15. This is due to the late arrival of the incoming plane. We apologise for any inconvenience this may cause.'

Israel barely heard the announcements. He was gazing out at the runway; his reflection in the darkness of the window, the weather outside whipping up to a storm, and the rain lashing down, peeling and splitting his face, his too solid and semi-permeable flesh fast disappearing in the blur.

He got up and bought a tray bake and a cup of coffee; food is always a great consolation in such circumstances. He might of course have been better off eating a freshly prepared salad, some steamed fish, and drinking some extract of wheat-grass, but unfortunately life is reality rather than fantasy, and the reality is that at half past nine on a Friday evening in the environs of Belfast City Airport, a tray bake and a cup of coffee are about the best that's on offer, just as self-pity – cheap, fattening and bad for the heart as undoubtedly it is – tends to be readily available around the clock and preferable to most alternatives. He took two sugars in the coffee – that faint tickling pain upon his receding gums – and he tried to remember what it was about Gloria.

He couldn't quite picture her face. When he tried to think about her he found he was thinking about other things, other people. He thought about Rosie. And he thought about his grandmother. He thought about the little Jack Russell pups. And Mr Wilson in his shed. He thought about that French photo, the one where the man wearing a scarf is leaning down to the woman's upturned face. And he thought of the scene in *Annie Hall* where Woody Allen and Diane Keaton meet outside her apartment and she invites him up and they're drinking wine on the balcony and enjoying pleasant conversation and the little thought bubbles pop up and you can see that Woody Allen is thinking, I wonder what she looks like naked.

He laughed to himself and sat on at the laminate table, his fingers greasy from the coffee and the caramel slice, just looking out of the window. Usually he'd have read a book.

At 10.30 he went down the stairs to wait by the exit.

The flight was announced; the flight arrived.

He thought for a moment that he recognised someone, but no. They were hurrying through to departures.

Passengers disembarked. Collected their luggage.

And Israel waited. And waited.

And the airport emptied.

He had a text.

'SPK,' said the message.

ACKNOWLEDGEMENTS

For previous acknowledgements see *The Truth About Babies* (Granta Books, 2002), *Ring Road* (Fourth Estate, 2004) and *The Mobile Library: The Case of the Missing Books* (Harper Perennial, 2006). These stand, with exceptions. In addition I would like to thank the following. (The previous terms and conditions apply: some of them are dead; most of them are strangers; the famous are not friends; none of them bears any responsibility.) To the editors of *The Enthusiast* – greetings.

Caroline Aherne, Arcade Fire, Arctic Monkeys, Tex Avery, David Bailey, Nancy Banks-Smith, Lynn Barber, Daniel Barenboim, Ronnie Barker, Brendan Barrington, Derek Beaven, Captain Beefheart, Catherine Bennett, Ambrose Bierce, St Blaise, Matthijs van Boxsel, Matthew Brady, British Sea Power, Charlie Brooker, Anne Brown, Ken Brown, Frank Bruno, James Lee Burke, Candace Bushnell, Andrea Camilleri, Karel Čapek, Frank Capra, Simon Carr, Michael Chabon, Martin Chambi, E.M. Cioran, Adam Coates, Rich Cohen, Jackie Collins, Joan Collins, Billy Connolly,

Cyril Connolly, Steve Coogan, Tommy Cooper, Sally Cotta, Thomas Cotta, Rob Cowan, Coyle's, Barry Cryer, Tom Dalzell, Jeff Daniels, Geena Davis, Kenneth C. Davis, Eve Dawson, Les Dawson, Mr Dawson, Guy Debord, Jack Dee, Daniel Dennett, Miss Derby, Mrs Dickson, Joan Didion, Norman Thomas Di Giovanni, Barry Douglas, Tim Dowling, St Eustachius, Simon Faithfull, Janet Flanner, George Foreman, St Francis, Nicolas Freeling, Dawn French, Ray Galton, Graeme Garden, James Geary, St Genesius, Boothby Graffoe, Blu Greenberg, Matt Groening, Andy Hamilton, Haruki Hartley, Mami Hartley, John Haskell, Simon Hoggart, Michael Holden, John Hollander, Eric Homberger, Pawel Huelle, Armando Iannucci, St Ignatius, Gary Imlach, Robert Irwin, Kay Redfield Jamison, Tove Jansson, Jack Johnson, Kaiser Chiefs, Dean Karnazes, Andy Kershaw, Florence King, Lizzy Kingston, St Lawrence, Sam Leith, William Leith, Emmanuel Levinas, Bernard Lewis, Victor Lewis-Smith, Walter Love, Humphrey Lyttleton, Emer McAfee, Alexander McCall Smith, Miss McClure, Mrs McCracken, Bill McGuire, Julian MacLaren Ross, Annabelle McNutt, Charles McNutt, Charlie McNutt, Charles McNutt, Mireille McNutt, Madonna, Janet Malcolm, Hilary Mantel, Andrew Martin, Willy Mason, David Matthews, Louis Menand, Andrew Miller, Daido Moriyama, Frank Muir, Arthur Mullard, Eadweard Muybridge, Carl Newbrook, Stephen Nolan, Martha O'Kane, Nicholas Ostler, Pierre Péju,

St Pelagia, Peter Perfrement, Bernard Perlin, Polar Bear, Tony Porter, Nicholas Rinaldi, David Rose, Jack Rosenthal, Josh Rouse, Tom Russell, Lorna Sage, Ryuichi Sakamoto, Mrs Sanders, Jennifer Saunders, Arthur Schopenhauer, Scrabo Audiology Unit, Sean, Dr Seuss, DJ Shantel, Neil Simon, Debbie Slater, Timothy Spall, Johnny Speight, Jim Steinmeyer, Alan Sugar, Matthew Sweet, Antal Szerb, Joel Taggart, Mrs Thompson, Paul Tillich, Sherill Tippins, P.L. Travers, Lionel Trilling, Mark Tully, Dubravka Ugresic, James Vanderzee, Terry Victor, Arthur Waley, Harriet Walter, Johnny Weismuller, Louise Welsh, Kanye West, Tim Westwood, Richard Williams, Frances Wilson, Terry Wogan, Steven Wright, *Your Place and Mine*, Carlos Ruiz Zafón.